'We marry, and bring Ross UK under the wide and accommodating umbrella of my company.'

Venetia straightened slowly. Six years ago she would have given all she possessed to hear Carlo propose marriage. And, even now, emotions she had thought to be buried deep in her memory flared to vibrant life, and it was some seconds before she felt composed enough to ask coolly, 'And the second option? It has to be better than the first.'

Dear Reader

As summer gives way to autumn, this is a good time to reflect on how you feel about your loved ones. Being in love can be the most wonderful feeling on earth, yet why is it that so many people are frightened of expressing that love? That's certainly the case between our hero and heroine, yet, as in life, once expressed, it can lead to the greatest happiness. I think there's a lot to be learned in our books. Have fun learning . . .!

The Editor

Diana Hamilton is a true romantic and fell in love with her husband at first sight. They still live in the fairy-tale Tudor house where they raised their three children. Now the idyll is shared with eight rescued cats and a puppy. But, despite an often chaotic lifestyle, ever since she learned to read and write Diana has had her nose in a book—either reading or writing one—and plans to go on doing just that for a very long time to come.

Recent titles by the same author:

SAVAGE OBSESSION
THREAT FROM THE PAST

LEGACY OF SHAME

BY

DIANA HAMILTON

MILLS & BOON

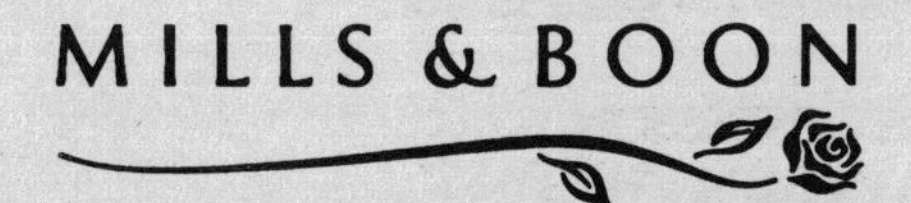

MILLS & BOON LIMITED
ETON HOUSE, 18-24 PARADISE ROAD
RICHMOND, SURREY TW9 1SR

First published in Great Britain 1993
by Mills & Boon Limited

This edition 1993

ISBN 0 263 78259 X

Set in Times Roman 10 on 12 pt.
01-9310-55520 C

Made and printed in Great Britain

CHAPTER ONE

VENETIA ADELE ROSS strode into the drawing-room without a thought in her head, the especially affectionate smile she reserved for her father curving her lush mouth, the pleasure of an afternoon's successful shopping spree making her pale blue eyes sparkle like fine crystal.

And then the world stood still. She actually felt it tilt on its axis and stop.

'Venny, darling, what kept you?'

No peevishness in the question, just warmth and affection. During the eighteen years of her life her father had never once chided her and meant it. She barely registered his voice, hardly saw him as he rose from his chair to walk to her side. And, for once, the room wasn't dominated by the huge oil portrait of the mother she'd lost when she was only a few months old. It was dominated instead by the man who had made the world stand still.

Carlo Rossi.

She had almost forgotten he was coming to visit, put it out of her mind, because the arrival, for a few weeks, of her father's cousin's unknown son hadn't put her in danger of dying from over-excitement!

And now this moment when time stood still gave her a sense of inevitability, a deeper understanding of fate than she had ever experienced before. A single second, such a tiny fragment of time, had been enough to face the shocking immediacy of meeting the one man she would love all her life, of falling in love, quite literally at first sight.

He was smiling at her across the width of the room. A smile that hovered between mannerliness and a kind of cynical interest. And her father was at her side now, taking her hand and giving it a small tug, as if he feared she'd grown roots into the Axminster-covered floor-boards, and he was saying, 'Come and say hello to Carlo, sweetheart.' She turned her black-fringed eyes to his, bewilderment reaching out to him as if he could solve this ancient enigma for her, as if it were a problem he could smooth away as he'd smoothed her path through life ever since she'd been born.

But this was no minor peccadillo; this was something major, beyond the control of a doting father's love and lavish financial generosity. Besides, he didn't know what had happened, did he? He didn't know how she was shaking inside her skin with the suddenness of it all, with the enormity, the shock of what had her rooted to the spot.

And his own bewilderment at her behaviour helped. He had no way of knowing why his normally confident, outgoing offspring looked as if she'd lost her wits. And his slightly impatient, 'Shake hands with your cousin,' had her smiling to herself, tugging all that confidence, the joy of living, the conviction that life was great, back into place. She set her long legs striding easily over the room, her smile frankly dazzling as Carlo Rossi held out a hand and disclaimed in a deep, slightly accented and thoroughly fascinating voice,

'As our fathers are merely cousins then our relationship is almost too remote to be significant.'

Venetia ignored the formally outstretched hand, but stood on tiptoe to brush a kiss on the side of his hard, tanned face instead, and did a little husky disclaiming of her own.

'In Italian families, any relationship, no matter how remote, is prized,' she said, and was astonished to find that he towered above her own five feet and ten inches, astonished moreover by how ultra-feminine she felt when she had to tilt back her head to meet his eyes. Heavily lidded, dark, magnificent eyes.

Steadying herself to impart that supposedly cousinly embrace, she had grasped his upper arms, and, even though she was now firmly back on the soles of her feet, she held on.

Venetia had a physical nature; she liked to touch, and the contact between the palms of her hands, the pads of her fingers and the warmth of the steel-hard muscles beneath the elegant pale grey suiting was little short of sensational.

Carlo Rossi was gorgeous! He stole away her breath, not to mention her heart! And never mind that a slightly sardonic tilt of one heavy dark brow accompanied the firm yet insistent pressure of his hands as he removed her clutching fingers, because one day she would hear him begging her to touch him, she vowed with an inner giggle she was at pains to suppress, her lush mouth curling provocatively as she enquired in the husky tones that were so uniquely her own, 'Has anything made any impact on you since your arrival?' her eyes teasing, challenging him to admit that she had! 'Though maybe it's a little soon,' she conceded with the smouldering pout, the Latin shrug that came from her Italian genes. 'It's your first time in England, isn't it?'

'Far from it. I know your country very well. I travelled extensively during my time here at university.' His answer was smooth and suave, and definitely cool, and she could have bitten her tongue out because she remembered, now, about some age-old rift between the two branches of the family. Not even something romantic like a feud over a woman, but some boring business thing.

Always highly perceptive where her father was concerned, she could sense his embarrassment over the forced admission that his cousin's son had visited before, had actually lived here for a time, and had not felt obliged to trouble himself to pay his respects. She wished the inane words unsaid, because upsetting her father was about the last thing she ever wanted to do.

'We'll be dining late this evening, Venny. So if you're ravenous, as usual, get Potty to give you some tea in the kitchen. And if I know you, you'll have half a ton of shopping littering up the hall.'

Her father's intervention had covered up her gaffe and the slight embarrassment it had presented, and she was thankful for that. But need he have emphasised her healthy young appetite quite so strongly? Not to mention the way she never seemed to know when to stop when she indulged her passion for shopping in London?

Her light-coloured eyes flicked sideways to Carlo, and sure enough he was smiling, merely a lazy curl at the corners of that sexy mouth, a slight glint of patronising amusement deep in the dark depths of his magnificent eyes. Enough to tell her, quite explicitly, that he was seeing her as a child who was not yet, not quite, boring him.

Trying to check an emotion that was nearer to rage than melting adoration, she murmured something about seeing him later and headed for the door. She'd show him, she fumed, closing the panelled wood with unnecessary force. She'd show him she wasn't a slightly amusing child!

Venetia was fully aware that she drew men's attention wherever she went, that admiring male eyes followed her on the street, in restaurants, at parties. And she knew that the few chaste kisses she'd allowed her carefully vetted escorts were not nearly enough for them, that they were greedy for much more. So what right had Carlo Rossi to look at her as if she were barely out of nappies!

He was, however, she had to concede as she stamped across the panelled hall that was fragrant with the scent of roses from the sprawling, picturesque garden, more of a man than most. He was everything that the escorts her father permitted were not. He was cultured, sophisticated, older—and dangerous.

Venetia shivered as something as wicked as it was scary lapped the length of her spine then churned around in her stomach. Carlo Rossi was like rare brandy after tepid cocoa!

Moreover, she could remember her father trying to work out the age of the cousin's son he hadn't seen since he'd worn short trousers. Thirty-one or -two. And he wasn't married, she knew that much, so he would hardly have got to that age without notching up more female conquests than was decent—not with his brand of heart-shattering looks, he wouldn't!

And his chosen female companions would not be teenagers—God, how she hated that twee appellation! They would be poised, as sophisticated as he, intelligent, independent women who didn't have appetites any navvy would be proud of, who dressed impeccably, in the best of taste, and were discreet enough not to leave a mountain of frivolous shopping cluttering up the floor space. Women who didn't screw their hair back in a plait, who wouldn't be seen dead in washed-out jeans and baggy T-shirt.

If only she had known she was about to be pole-axed by the very sight of him, she would have shot upstairs to change into something more alluring and released her waist-length hair and brushed it until it resembled a fall of jet-black silk, she mourned, her confidence deserting her for the first time in her life, leaving her feeling uncharacteristically unsure of herself, and quite miserable.

But the untidy mound of classy carriers and boxes did something to restore it. She had practically cleaned out her allowance, but she had bought some utterly delicious things! And she had plenty of time before dinner to make herself over, appear before him at her most glamorous. She had always managed to get whatever she wanted before, able to twist her doting father round the end of her little finger.

And she wanted Carlo Rossi.

And she would get him, too!

Without any help from her father, because this was something she would enjoy doing all by herself!

She was halfway up the stairs, boxes sliding this way and that as she desperately clutched at them with carrier-laden hands, when she met Mrs Potts coming down. A short, comfortably curved woman, her placid nature allowed her to take any crisis in her stride. She had become Venetia's father's housekeeper after her mother's tragic death, and as soon as Venetia had begun to talk she had named her Potty, and it had stuck.

'Let me help.' Potty took the teetering layer of boxes and headed back up the stairs, dumping them on Venetia's crimson satin-covered bed. 'Been spending another fortune, by the look of it.'

'You know I can't resist.' Venetia disregarded the token grumble in the older woman's tone. Like Venetia's father, Potty was a push-over; she had learned to twist them both around her tiny fingers before she'd begun to toddle. 'Besides, I found the most fantastic dress.' She opened one of the larger boxes and fished out a slither of black silk. 'What do you think? Isn't it just the sexiest thing you ever saw? And isn't it fortuitous? Just the thing to knock Carlo's eyes out!'

'Looks more like a petticoat, if you ask me,' the housekeeper disapproved. 'Scarcely decent. And that cousin of yours is far too old and sensible to take any notice of what you wear. So don't waste your efforts. Now——' having said her piece, she turned back to the door '—how about a nice cup of tea and a slice or two of my chocolate cake? You can have it in the kitchen and tell me what else you've wasted your father's money on while I do the veggies for dinner.'

Just for a moment, Venetia was sorely tempted. No one made chocolate cake like Potty did, and she'd enjoy a good gloat over her varied purchases, and lunch did seem a long time ago... But, 'No, thanks, Potty. I'll just get this lot unpacked and take a bath,' she resisted firmly.

At the moment, her figure could justifiably be described as luscious, but if she didn't curb her appetite she could end up as just plain fat! She smiled seraphically into Potty's astonished face and turned to do her unpacking.

If falling in love could give her the will-power to turn down the offer of great wodges of deliciously wicked chocolate cake then love had to be, as many a ballad-maker had proclaimed, a sweet miracle indeed!

But it had its serious side, too, and could frighten her a little if she let it, she admitted as she luxuriated later in a lavishly scented bath. She knew she'd been pampered and petted all her life, but when her father did put his foot down he really meant it, and no amount of wheedling and coaxing on her part would make him change his mind.

Which was why her dates had been limited, her escorts carefully vetted. And, coupled with her expensive education at a girls' convent school where the nuns' zealous strictness had meant that even the most inventive and headstrong of the pupils had not been able to step out of line for one moment, Venetia was woefully inexperienced, her sexuality a complete mystery.

Nothing had prepared her for the way Carlo Rossi made her feel, for the way her heart twisted and leapt inside her when she looked at him, performing acrobatic somersaults even when she only thought of him!

And the sweet-sharp melting sensation which was afflicting her entire body right now as she lay in the warm water picturing their next meeting, when she would appear as a sensual woman and not as a pigtailed, overlarge schoolgirl, was totally new to her, ragingly exciting and definitely a little frightening.

Not even Simon Carew, her most regular escort, who made his sexual interest in her plainer than most when they were alone together, had come near to rousing these deliciously wicked sensations within her.

Simon, at twenty-five, was sharp as a needle and undeniably attractive in his blond Anglo-Saxon way. Recently promoted to the position of her father's personal assistant in the family-owned wine, shipping and retail business, he was her usual escort to those parties and first nights her father had no inclination to attend.

Her father trusted Simon completely. He would have forty fits if he knew how often his blue-eyed boy had tried to seduce his precious daughter.

What he didn't understand was that she could take care of herself, that she'd had no trouble deflecting Simon's amorous advances. She just wasn't interested, not even when he'd mentioned marriage, and had told him so. And she certainly wouldn't dream of telling her father where Simon's interests lay, because his duties as escort would have ceased at once, leaving her kicking her heels at home while he vetted and checked out some other young man.

She could handle herself, she thought, a complacent smile curling her mouth as she stepped out of the bath in a shower of watery droplets and reached for one of the thick white towels. But complacency vanished on a shudder of exquisite excitement as she recalled the smouldering depths of Carlo's magnificent eyes. She wouldn't even try to take care of herself if those deep, dark eyes warmed to passion! If Carlo Rossi attempted to seduce her she would abandon all those moral principles that had been drummed into her head and wholeheartedly do all she could to encourage him!

Dressing for dinner was almost impossible given the state she was in. Her whole body was trembling with liquid excitement, seeming to have no more substance than an ill-set jelly, her fingers all thumbs and her legs mere columns of cotton wool.

Having mangled two pairs of sheer black silk stockings, Venetia pulled her mind together and, instead of concentrating on the amazing sensations she'd been experiencing since setting eyes on the dark Italian, turned over the facts as she knew them.

During the run-up to Carlo's visit her father had often spoken of the Italian branch of the family, and Venetia, dutifully, had listened, pretending an interest she certainly hadn't felt. But now the facts were vitally important; everything pertaining to Carlo was suddenly utterly riveting!

Over a hundred years ago the family wine-exporting business had been split, her great-grandfather coming to England to found the import and retail side. Since then, her branch of the family had been anglicised, and, as the retail outlets had proliferated, so had the wine-shipping side of the business.

But the Italian Rossis had prospered too, maintaining a forty-nine-per-cent interest in the British company while expanding and diversifying themselves, acquiring ever more vineyards, both in Italy and France, vast acres of rich farmland around Valencia and luxury hotels in every major city in the world.

Which would make Carlo infinitely wealthier and far more powerful than her own father, she mused. Particularly since, from what she recalled of her father's conversations, Carlo's father was ailing, had been for the past few years, leaving Carlo himself practically, if not nominally, in charge of the vast Rossi empire.

Furthermore, Carlo's visit was an olive-branch, a means of ending the family feud which had existed since her father had been a boy, hinging on a disputed package of shares in the UK side of the business. It would be really dreamy, she decided with an ecstatic wriggle of inner excitement, if she and Carlo, respectively the last of the two branches of the family, were to marry and so begin the foundation of a once-more united dynasty!

And it wasn't impossible, was it?

Standing back and viewing her reflection in the full-length mirror, she assured herself that it was completely, utterly, gloriously possible!

For this evening she had chosen to leave her silky straight waist-length hair loose, caught back from the sides of her face with gilded combs, and her heavier than usual use of make-up emphasised the creamy skin that never seemed to tan, the thickness of her sweeping dark lashes and the luscious pout of her full mouth.

And the new, outrageously expensive dress was well worth every penny, she thought, noting how the fine black silk clung so lovingly to every ripe curve, the short length of the skirt revealing the elegance of endless black silk-clad legs, the tiny shoe-string straps and scoopy bodice emphasising the wide milky-white shoulders and generously full breasts of a woman who was in full bloom, totally feminine, and proud of it!

Tonight, Carlo Rossi wouldn't be seeing her as an overgrown teenager—on that she would stake her life!

The unstoppable self-confidence of one to whom everything in life came easily had her practically floating down the staircase on expensively nonsensical shoes which were a mere cat's-cradle of gold kid wispy straps and impossibly slender high heels, and the bubbly excitement that made her feel as if she were intoxicated on the finest champagne didn't subside by the merest notch when she found Potty to be the sole occupant of the elegantly yet comfortably furnished drawing-room.

'Your father's in the library with his guest and I shouldn't think they'll show their faces until dinner. And don't you think you should cover up with a cardigan or something?'

'Cardigan?' Venetia scoffed affectionately. 'How old-fashioned can you get?' The housekeeper had been refilling the heavy Georgian sherry decanter, and Venetia helped herself to a glass. 'Anyway, it's a beautiful evening. I'm not in the least bit cold.'

'I'm not worried about the temperature,' Potty snorted, eyeing the generous dose of sherry Venetia had given herself with the same disapproval she had given the slinky dress. 'You're not decent, that's the long and short of it. What your poor father will think, not to mention your cousin, I shudder to imagine! That—that thing you're wearing shows everything you've got!'

Which was precisely what it was meant to do, Venetia thought with a wicked smile that made her eyes sparkle like clear, pure rain-water as she ignored Potty's continued grumbles and took herself and her sherry out through the French windows and on to the paved terrace.

The warm evening air was rich with the scent of roses and touched her skin with the softness of a lover's caress, making her tremble with the renewed onslaught of emotions that were entirely new to her. And the sight of the open French windows to the library, further along the terrace, was too much for her self-control.

Never before would she have dreamed of interrupting her father when he was in a business or private discussion; she had far too much respect for him. But her need to feast her eyes on the superlative masculinity that was Carlo Rossi, to allow him to see her as a mature and desirable woman, was too strong to resist right now.

The height of her heels and the tightness of her skirt made her curvaceous hips sway with unself-conscious sexual provocation as she walked through from the terrace into the book-lined room, a slow smile tilting her lush mouth, her eyes half veiled by thick black lashes as she chided huskily, 'The evening's too beautiful to waste indoors. Won't you let me show you the gardens, Carlo?'

Her eyes met his with taunting challenge, her heart skipping several beats as he rose from the shabby leather chesterfield. He, too, had dressed for dinner, and he looked sensational, the formal black jacket and crisp white linen shirt suiting his dark, predatory looks to perfection. And for one long moment those magnificent black eyes searched hers, alert with tacit questions, then glittered darkly as his hard mouth softened to something that was almost a smile, an answer to her own unspoken challenge.

On the periphery of her vision she saw her father rise from the chair behind his huge leather-topped desk, sensed his disapproval at her unprecedented interruption, perhaps—who knew?—guessing at her reason for it, and dismissed him from her mind, hearing only the silence, sensing only the guarded drift of Carlo's eyes as they appraised the voluptuous curves beneath the thin black satin.

'Why not?' He dipped his sleek dark head, not quickly enough to hide the dent of amusement at the side of his mouth, before turning to her father. 'Perhaps you will join us, sir? It is, as Venetia says, a beautiful evening.'

Don't! Venetia pleaded fiercely inside her head. Having her father tag along wasn't part of her plans!

Then she exhaled the breath she hadn't realised she'd been holding as the older man said slowly, 'No, you two go ahead.' And then, more briskly, 'Be sure to show Carlo the water garden, Venny. And don't forget the time. Potty will be serving dinner in under an hour.'

'I won't,' Venetia assured, the radiance of her smile undimmed by her parent's faint, puzzled frown as she stepped to Carlo's side and tucked her hand beneath his arm and led him out on to the terrace.

After the cool, almost cloistered atmopshere of the library, the early evening sun on her naked arms and shoulders brought a sybaritic smile to her glossy lips and her eyes drifted shut for an instant of sensual pleasure, the deep tones of his voice sending a *frisson* of delight right through her, even though his words were vaguely patronising in content.

'Wouldn't you prefer to leave your glass behind? You can drink your sherry later; no one's going to steal it from you.'

As if she were a child who couldn't be persuaded to part with a sticky lollipop! But Venetia refused to be put down. Pausing at the top of the steps that led down from the terrace, she gave him her most dazzling smile and told him huskily, 'You can steal anything of mine, any time you please.' She placed the rim of the glass to her pouting lips, her pale, translucent eyes smouldering between thickly fringing lashes as she touched the tip of her tongue to the cool crystal. 'But why don't we share?' She took a long swallow of the pale, aromatic liquid then slowly lifted the glass to his strangely unsmiling mouth. And he drained it as if he had no option, as if it were an inescapable ritual, his eyes never leaving the pure, almost imperiously beautiful lines of her face as she watched the controlled ripple of his throat as he drank, her fingertips aching to follow the track of her fascinated gaze.

'The water garden, then.' The incisive cut of his voice broke the spell of that strangely ritualistic bonding, as if he were making some violent repudiation. And she shrugged slightly, hating this new sensation of uncertainty, watching from clouded eyes as he set the glass carefully on top of the stone balustrading and descended the steps.

Venetia jerked herself together and followed. But too quickly, one of her ridiculous heels twisting beneath her in her haste.

But what she lost in dignity she gained in the exquisite sanctuary of his arms as he caught and steadied her, holding her warm, soft body against the steel-hard litheness of his, and for a timeless moment she knew what heaven on earth must feel like. She was melting into him, completing him, just as he was making her truly whole. He was her other half, her *alter ego*, and the recognition made her giddy.

'You're hardly dressed for out of doors, I think.'

The steel in his voice was only just covered in silk and he was putting her aside, his hands firm; she recovered her equilibrium enough to tell him lightly, 'Nonsense. It's just a stroll. I caught my heel in a crack between the stones. Too silly!' And she grabbed his arm with a firmness that almost matched his own and set out along the gravelled walkway.

She could sense his withdrawal, the deliberate remoteness he was using like a shield, but it didn't really bother her. Why should it, when he could have turned back to the house, refused to go along with the pretext of seeing the grounds? But he hadn't refused, beat a tactical retreat, she exulted. He kept right beside her, not even brushing her hand away from his arm, slowing his long-legged stride to accommodate her shorter steps.

So he could look as remote as he liked. She smiled softly to herself as she glanced at the proud, stern lines of his profile; he wasn't fooling her! She had witnessed the awakening of something far more than cousinly interest when he'd made that thorough appraisal of her body, and she'd felt the magic chemistry that had made her feel they were one flesh when he'd briefly held her in his arms. It had been too strong, too blindingly insistent for him to have been unaware of it.

'Nearly there,' she said, her voice smoky, breaking the silence, reflecting that he'd been right when he'd said she wasn't dressed for out of doors. Short, tight skirts and impossible heels were hardly suitable for traversing even the most carefully raked gravelled paths or the most smoothly kept lush green lawns. 'How long will you be staying?' she asked, her fingers tightening around his iron-hard arm as they descended mossy stone steps beneath a deep arch in the high yew hedge which separated the grounds.

'One week. Two. Who knows?' The upward shift of his wide shoulders was eloquently, fluidly dismissive, but she ignored it. If he was pretending he wasn't aware of her then she could pretend she hadn't noticed the subterfuge!

'Plenty of time for me to show you around,' she stated, her eyes gleaming up at his impassive features as she pictured long walks into the countryside, intimate dinners for two at secluded restaurants, maybe even a drive into the Welsh mountains where she could successfully lose them in all that wildness, maybe for long enough to necessitate an overnight stay at some remote farmhouse...

'You are not studying, at school maybe? Or working?'

He waited politely as she hopped down from the final and deepest stone step and, that obstacle negotiated, she answered airily, 'School? Good lord, no!' She managed to convey that her schooldays were a dim and distant memory, not prepared to tell him that her final term had ended a scant three weeks ago and so remind him of her age. 'Look—we're here,' she told him unnecessarily as they entered the grotto filled with the scent and sound of water.

But he didn't appear to be remotely interested in the water garden. His dark eyes gave her a cool glance as he questioned, 'Do you plan a career? Within the company, perhaps?'

'Oh, who knows?' Venetia frowned, biting down on her full lower lip. 'Let's not talk about that.' Why waste time discussing the possibility of a career in her father's business when all she wanted to do was spend the rest of her life with him? And she did want that, want it with a sudden desperation that left her feeling devastated.

Hesitantly, she searched his eyes and found nothing there but cold disinterest. A pain, like a splinter of ice, stabbed at her heart. He didn't even like her. Had she lived through her life, effortlessly receiving everything she'd ever wanted, only to be denied the most important, the thing she craved above all else?

Venetia shivered, cold to her bones as shameful tears stung the backs of her eyes. And Carlo stated, a curl of cynical amusement playing around his mouth, 'This place is dank. You should have worn your mink. I take it you do own a couple, at least?'

'Half a dozen at last count!' she snapped back at him, stung to immediate, hurting rage by his patronising, cynical, coolly mocking attitude. She wouldn't demean herself by explaining she wouldn't be seen dead in a fur, that she passionately believed they looked better on the animals they were designed to grace!

The emotional turmoil she'd experienced since setting eyes on him had turned to passionate hatred. She wanted to hit him, but contained the violence, curling her fingers into her palms until the painted nails dug deeply into the soft flesh. And she met the intimidating censure of his narrowed eyes with open hostility until raw pain sliced through her, the sensation of the wounding mirrored in the translucent depths of her eyes as she lowered them, blinking back the scalding flow of tears.

She hadn't meant it to be like this. Oh, she surely hadn't! And she was cold again now. So cold. Nothing really to do with the moist, shaded air, the watery silence of the quiet pool, the moss-grown rocks, the still, heavy leaves of the gunnera and ornamental rhubarb—nothing to do with them at all.

Venetia turned quickly, the silky fall of her hair flying around her shoulders as she tottered as rapidly as she could back towards the steps, her heart leaping inside her, her throat closing with solidified breath as he stopped her, his large hands on her shoulders swinging her round to face him.

'You'll break your neck if you go at that pace, or, at the very least, spoil your pretty shoes.' His voice went husky as he watched the play of emotions cross her pale features, saw them spring to tumultuous life in the translucent depths of her beautiful eyes.

'I...' Venetia tried to speak, but couldn't. And her lashes lowered as his hands gentled, the pads of his fingers lightly massaging the tender, responsive flesh below her collarbone.

'I didn't mean to upset you,' he said, his voice rough, his mouth compressed. His fingers slid upwards, slowly, resting against the long, pure line of her throat. And she felt the tremor take hold of his lean body, ripple through him, and the words she would have said dried again in her throat.

Fluttering, her long lashes drifted upwards, and what she saw in those dark, hooded eyes made her heart stand still. Slowly the tip of her tongue moistened her parched lips, and she saw him close his eyes, heard the raw sound he made deep in his throat, and melted towards him instinctively, her hands splaying against his chest, nudging aside the elegant jacket to feel the warmth of his body beneath the thin covering of crisp linen, feel the heavy beat of his heart. Then she heard the rough intake of his breath as he gently set her aside and said unevenly, 'We'll be late for dinner. Come along, now, there's a good girl.'

And Venetia tilted her head and gave him a long, lancing glance of triumph, gave him her bewitching smile before demurely falling in step beside him. He might treat her as if she were a child. But that wasn't the way his body reacted to her at all!

And soon, very soon now, she would insinuate herself beneath his guard and make him admit that he wanted her just as much as she wanted him!

CHAPTER TWO

But it wasn't easy. Carlo Rossi had a will of iron. Days passed, and then a full week had gone by, and he had turned down all her sightseeing suggestions with that slight, ironic smile, preferring, obviously, to spend time with her father at head office, returning with him in the evening, leaving Venetia kicking her heels at home, fuming.

And over the long, unhurried dinners that had lasted well into the amethyst evenings he'd kept his conversation with her to a polite minimum, and when he wasn't discussing business with her father he talked of his homeland, reminding the older man of his forsaken roots.

But Venetia hadn't given up hope. On a few occasions she'd turned and surprised the hooded, hungry look in his eyes, and known that he was deliberately erecting a wall between them, and set herself the problem of how to break through it.

On some deeply primitive masculine level he did want her, she knew it. She'd seen the need smouldering darkly in his fantastic eyes, catching him unawares, her own need leaping to match his before he'd pulled the shutters down, locking her out with a tiny derisive smile, the hunger masked by a blank indifference that made her want to throw back her head and howl, stamp her feet with frustration.

Because every day that passed, every hour, reinforced her love, her wanting. Nothing else mattered; her need of him had bitten deep into her psyche, expanding until it filled her whole being. And for the first time in her life she was not being given what she wanted!

'Phone, for you.' Potty trundled out on to the terrace, where Venetia was kicking her heels, furious because, early as she had risen, pulling on a pair of shorts and a sleeveless T-shirt, Carlo had beaten her to it.

Today was Saturday and he wouldn't be going in to the office with her father, and she'd been determined to persuade him to spend time with her, walking, making use of the swimming-pool, anything.

But when she'd arrived downstairs the housekeeper had told her that Carlo had set out on foot an hour ago to 'see something of the countryside', and she'd been out here ever since, cursing herself for sleeping until seven when, if she'd surfaced an hour earlier, she could have set out with him. The man was impossible! How could she break down that wall if he refused to stay still long enough to give her the opportunity to try?

Her mind, as usual, totally preoccupied with thoughts of Carlo Rossi, she took the call in the library, frowning impatiently as Simon said in his light, pleasant voice, 'Sorry to call you at the crack, but I wanted to confirm the time for tonight.'

'Tonight?' Venetia echoed blankly, hooking a strand of long silky hair behind a small, perfectly shaped ear, and Simon reminded amusedly,

'Your friend's eighteenth birthday party, remember? What time shall I pick you up?'

'Oh, that.' She had forgotten all about Natasha's coming-of-age celebrations. Normally, she wouldn't have missed it for a king's ransom. But circumstances weren't normal. Nothing could drag her away, no matter how glittering the party, while there was the remotest chance of spending time with Carlo. 'I've changed my mind,' she said. 'I'm not going.' Then, because the silence on the other end of the line was speaking volumes, she tacked on, 'I'm sorry, I should have let you know earlier. But we have a house guest. I'm fully occupied keeping him entertained . . .' Oh, would that that were true! 'You must have met him. Carlo Rossi . . .' Even the sound of his name on her tongue sent hungry yearnings skittering through her, and she went on breathlessly, 'He's been following my father to the office each day.'

'Hardly following.' Simon gave a short, humourless laugh. 'Dragging everyone behind him is more like it! He's turned the distribution network upside-down, gone through the accounts with a magnifying glass, and got everyone working in top gear.'

'Can he do that?' Venetia queried, her eyes shining. She didn't doubt his ability to take complete and total charge wherever he was. His aura of domination, of utter self-assurance, had been one of the many characteristics that had made such an immediate impact on her. But she asked the question all the same because, apart from feasting her eyes on him, talking about him was her favourite occupation.

'You'd better believe it,' Simon told her drily. 'His father handed over his forty-nine per cent of the shares in Ross UK to him, and that gives him a whole lot of clout. But, that apart, he's a natural top dog; one look at him is enough to make anyone with any sense toe the line! Mind you,' he added grudgingly, 'his organisational abilities come out of the top drawer, you can't argue with that. He sees solutions to problems before the rest of we lesser mortals recognise there's a problem at all.'

Venetia could have listened to this kind of thing for hours, but Simon had other ideas.

'Are you sure about tonight? It could be a whole load of fun, and we could go on to a nightclub later, just the two of us,' he coaxed. 'The old man doesn't need to know what time we leave your friend's birthday party.'

'Get lost!' Venetia pulled a face at the receiver before crashing it down.

Simon was getting too uppity. He must know she tolerated his sexual come-ons, parrying them with firm good humour, only because to refuse to have anything more to do with him socially would mean she'd be stuck at home missing out on all the fun until her father came up with a replacement escort he felt he could trust with his precious offspring!

But if he was starting to refer to her father as 'the old man' in that disrespectful tone, suggesting they deceive him, then she was prepared to slap him down in no uncertain manner and stay home every night into the foreseeable future!

Besides, she thought as she hunched her shoulders and wandered listlessly out of the room, Carlo was the only man she wanted to be with. The trouble was, he was making it clear that he had no wish to be with her!

And then she stopped right in the middle of the huge hall as the perfect idea hit her. It was so perfect—it couldn't be faulted!

A smile curved her full lips, her eyes sparkling with the resurgence of the confidence that had gone missing for days. And she turned as the housekeeper walked in through the front door, leaving it open so that the warm morning sunlight streamed in. She had been cleaning the lion's head doorknocker, dusters and metal polish in her hands, and Venetia bit back a bubble of excitement and asked, 'Did Carlo say what time he'd be back?'

'He didn't say and I didn't ask,' the older woman said drily. 'But I dare say he'll show up in time for lunch.' She drew level, settling the wooden box that held her cleaning materials more securely under her arm. 'So I shouldn't waste the morning hanging around for him, if I were you. And a word of advice——' her round face went as stern as it was possible to get '—don't make your crush on him so obvious. You'll soon get over it and when you do you'll feel a fool. You'll regret the way you've been hanging around him.' Then, at the flash of pure fury in Venetia's pale eyes, her expression softened as she added, 'It's your pride that will hurt most in the end, pet. I can understand the attraction; what woman couldn't? But apart from him being too old for you, he's probably got half a dozen or so elegant ladies waiting for him back home. Now——' the lecture over, she glanced at the long-case clock on the wall '—it's gone half-past nine; has your father come down yet? It's not like him to lie in this late, is it?'

'I haven't seen him,' Venetia responded icily. How dared Potty call what she felt for Carlo a crush! She wasn't a child. She loved Carlo and always would. And what would Potty know about it? She was fifty if she was a day!

Swinging round on her heels, her shoulders huffily rigid, she marched to the main door, dragging the summer-scented air through pinched nostrils. No one understood how she was hurting, how her need to get close to Carlo both spiritually and physically was an ache that grew larger every day because he simply wouldn't let her through the wall he had deliberately erected around himself.

It was going to be hot, she decided, feeling the sun burn against her exposed skin as she wandered out on to the drive. Normally, on a day like today was going to be, she would have happily idled away several hours in or beside the outdoor swimming-pool. But she was too restless to even contemplate it, even though the heat seemed to be growing more sultry with every moment that passed.

Besides, she needed to see Carlo; she couldn't run the risk of missing him on his return. She had formulated the perfect plan to get him to herself, and he couldn't refuse, surely he couldn't?

Settling down on the last of the stone steps that led to the main door, she leant against the plinth that carried an urn which billowed with scarlet geraniums, breathing in their spicy scent and determined to stay exactly where she was until she took root, if necessary, then saw that she wouldn't have to wait that long because Carlo was already approaching the house along the drive.

Her heart beating rapidly enough to choke her, she scrambled to her feet and tried to look cool and calm. Everything depended on how she extended the invitation. She had to put it in a way that would make it impossible for him to turn down, make him feel that he would be behaving discourteously as a guest in her father's home if he were to do so.

It was the first time she had seen him in anything but lightweight, impeccably elegant business suits or formal evening wear and, if anything, he looked even more impossibly attractive in slim-fitting tan-coloured cotton jeans topped by an open-necked black shirt. Come to me; love me as I love you! she commanded desperately inside her head, then, as she felt the helpless tears suddenly glaze her eyes, she blinked them back and hauled herself together.

Slowly, she began to walk towards him, trying to look as if she had nothing more important on her mind than the enjoyment of the glorious weather. But inside she was a mess. Her heart was beating thickly, suffocating her, her breathing going haywire, because if he refused to agree to her request she would know she had lost the only remaining chance she had to get him to fall in love with her a little.

Desperately she reminded herself that there was no room in her head for thoughts of failure, and deliberately avoided looking directly at him as they met. She turned her head instead to contemplate the façade of the house as she swung on her heels and fell in step beside him.

'Enjoy your walk?' She kept her voice cool, devoid of anything but polite interest, and that was good. And successfully fought the temptation to reach.out and hold on to his arm, even though her fingers ached to touch that firm, sun-warmed, tanned flesh.

'Very much.' His response was terse. If he was pleased to see her he wasn't showing it. 'Is your father around? I need to speak to him.'

'I haven't seen him this morning.' Vaguely she recalled Potty remarking on his lateness, and quickly dismissed the thought from her head, because this whole scenario looked like running away from her.

Carlo had increased his stride and she was having to trot to keep up with him, and nothing was going as she'd planned it in her head.

'Would you do me a favour?' The words came out in a breathless gabble, the sophisticated, almost bored approach she'd decided on nowhere in sight, because he was making for the house as if the hounds of hell were on his tail!

And then he seemed to freeze; she could see the wide, rangy shoulders stiffen as he slowly turned to face her, his stunning features perfectly blank as he assured her with formal politeness, 'Naturally. If I can.'

Suddenly, the butterflies in her stomach became a flock of crazed eagles, and she almost turned and fled, and had to force herself to stay right where she was.

'Well?' The indifferent enquiry was accompanied by a small, hard smile as he thrust his thumbs into the side pockets of his trousers and rocked indolently back on his heels.

'I...' All those carefully planned words had fallen out of her head and, to steady herself, she took a deep breath and watched in a kind of wondering triumph when his hooded eyes dropped to her breasts as the long gulp of air into her lungs thrust them against the soft fabric of her skimpy top.

He was aware of her. He was! As much as he tried to hide it from her, and possibly from himself, these were the tiny, give-away signs that had stopped her from abandoning all hope days ago!

And she said, only a little shakily, 'Well, actually, a friend of mine is having a birthday party at the Savoy tonight. I said I'd go, and you know how it is——' she managed a slight shrug '—I don't want to disappoint her. But Father has this bee in his bonnet about letting me loose on my own, and I wondered if you could do me a favour and act as my escort?'

She held her breath, willing him to agree, and all the time she watched his face, her eyes wide with unknowing entreaty, the tip of her tongue nervously flickering between her lips as she watched his mouth tighten, his nostrils flare just briefly, before he coolly informed her, 'I'm sure the party will be delightful. However, as I'm leaving for Rome tomorrow my time will be fully occupied this evening.'

She stared at him with shocked, bewildered eyes. Two body-blows in one cruel sentence. Not only had he refused her request, but he was leaving the country tomorrow. How could she stand it? She hated herself for being so vulnerable, hated him for being the cause of all this pain. And heard him say, a strange softness in his voice, 'Try to forgive me, Venetia. In a little while, a few weeks—days, even—you will forget all this——' he shrugged eloquent shoulders, his face softening, his smile crooked as he found the words he wanted '—this infatuation. I am too old for you, too hard and, most probably, too intolerant.' He lifted his beautiful, strong hands, as if he was about to touch her, then dropped them back to his sides, his brows drawing together in a frown that told her something was irritating him. Her, most probably! And she scarcely registered what he said, an unusual curtness clipping his tone. 'You are young and exquisitely lovely. Go to your party tonight and enjoy yourself with people your own age. Forget you ever asked me. I certainly will. Believe me, it could have been the biggest mistake either one of us is ever likely to make.'

'I hate you!' Colour came and went in her face, tears of rage spiking her lashes, trembling there before falling, streaking her cheeks and dripping off the end of her elegant nose. And she didn't care. He knew how she felt about him and had denigrated it as a schoolgirlish infatuation, given her tattered emotions about as much concern as he would extend if she'd caught a head cold! Over and forgotten in a few days—nothing that couldn't be cured by a few doses of fun with a few other juveniles! She couldn't be more humiliated than that! And she repeated ferociously, 'God, how I hate you!'

'Then you must be heartily relieved that I didn't take you up on your invitation, mustn't you?' His smile was sheer, infuriating irony. 'And I'm sure young Carew could be prevailed upon to escort you this evening. Although if I were you I'd take care where he's concerned; he's a chancer, and I don't think he's entirely to be trusted, even though your father appears to do so—enough to pay him handsomely to chaperon you!'

His black eyes impaled her, as they were no doubt meant to do, and she went cold with the shock of discovering how hateful he could be.

He had set out to humiliate her and had effortlessly succeeded. How could he lie like that, say that Simon had to be paid to take her out? Was he trying to tell her that no man in his right mind would be seen with her unless he was paid to do so? She didn't believe him; she couldn't! And she dashed the tears from her face with the tips of her fingers as she flung at him grittily, 'I wonder if you know how vile you really are! Do you always get your kicks out of hurting people?'

His reply was lost beneath the crunch of gravel as she ran back to the house, and she was too emotionally ragged as she entered the hall to notice her father until his thready voice burst through the pounding in her head. 'Venny, now don't worry, sweetheart, but could you call Dr Fielding?'

Venetia's heart gave a massive, painful thump as her eyes flew to her father. He was standing at the foot of the stairs, leaning against the newel post, still in his dressing-gown, his face grey and slicked with perspiration.

'Daddy! What's wrong?' The question was torn from her as she ran to him, picking up one of his hands and holding it against her cheek, fear in her wide, water-clear eyes.

'Probably nothing more serious than a stomach-ache.' His wan smile was meant to reassure her but it did nothing of the kind, and for the first time in a week she wasn't aware of Carlo's presence, hadn't realised he'd followed her into the house until he spoke behind her, his voice calm.

'Phone, Venetia. At once.'

Reluctantly, she dropped her father's hand, stepping back on legs that felt distinctly unsteady, her eyes flying up to Carlo's impassive features, willing him to tell her everything would be all right.

But he wasn't looking her way, his eyes assessing the elderly man before lifting him effortlessly into his arms, still not looking at her as he commanded, 'I said at once, Venetia.'

Guiltily, she ran over to the phone, her fingers shaking as she punched in the numbers of the surgery, gnawing on the corner of her mouth as she waited for the receiver to be lifted at the other end. And her incoherent babblings must have made some sense because the receptionist said that Dr Fielding was as good as on his way, and she turned away, butting into Potty, who was now standing directly behind her, her eyes anxious in her parchment-pale face.

'Is he coming?' she asked quickly, and Venetia nodded, her throat too choked with fear to allow her to speak.

'Good. That's all right, then.' The housekeeper visibly relaxed, as if she was convinced that all the doctor had to do was wave a prescription. Venetia wished she had such blind, unquestioning faith. She couldn't forget how desperately ill her father had looked.

And something of this must have shown in her face, because Potty stroked a strand of silky black hair away from her clammy forehead, her voice reassuring as she soothed, 'It won't be long before the doctor gets here, and Carlo's with him. He took him to the library and asked me to fetch a blanket. Run along, now; go and hold his hand, why don't you?'

Venetia tried to pull herself together as she watched the older woman hurry to complete her errand. It wouldn't help her father if she appeared at his side looking distraught. And somehow, clinging on to the thought that Carlo was with him helped her. Nothing bad could happen while he was there. He wouldn't let it!

Nothing this traumatic had happened to her in her entire life and she'd been young enough, inexperienced enough—until ten minutes ago—to believe it never would.

She had been only a few months old when her mother had died. The horse she had been riding had fallen at a gate, crushing the life out of the slender young woman. Venetia had been unaware of the tragedy, and her father had done all he could to ensure that she never felt the lack of a maternal parent too keenly. He had, all her life, lavished enough love, care and patience on her for two.

She remembered now the look on his face when, at the age of eleven, she had asked for a pony of her own. At the time, she hadn't translated that haunted expression as fear. It hadn't been until years later, when her undoubted equestrian skills had led her to take calculated risks, that she had finally put two and two together, tying the look of agony deep in his kindly eyes to the tragic death of her mother.

Parting with Bliss, her lovely grey mare, had been the hardest thing she had ever had to do; convincing her father that she was giving up riding because the sport was beginning to bore her had called upon all her acting abilities.

But it had been worth it for the look of soul-deep relief in his eyes. It had been the first completely unselfish act of her young life and she prayed it wouldn't be her last.

She felt guilty as she recalled how, a full year before she had been due to leave the convent school, she had flatly refused to make any plans for future career training, and, when the time had come for her to wipe the cloistered dust of the convent from her feet, had brushed aside her father's suggestion that she join the family business, working her way through every department right up to the top.

What she had wanted, she had lovingly teased him, was to stay home and have fun for at least six months before having to think of anything as dreary as working for her living. After the nuns' stern discipline she had deserved that much, hadn't she?

She knew she had disappointed him, although he had tried not to let it show. And now she regretted her frivolous attitude to life more keenly than she would ever have believed possible.

Potty caught up with her as she reached the library door, pushing a folded blanket into her arms.

'Take this to him, while I wait around to show the doctor through,' she instructed. 'Then I'll make us all a nice cup of tea. I dare say you could do with one. I know I could.'

Consciously relaxing her shoulders, Venetia pushed open the library door, giving a terse nod at Carlo's, 'Well, is he on his way?'

'How are you feeling now?' she wanted to know as she tucked the blanket around her father's legs. He was stretched out on the chesterfield and he smiled at her.

'Better. Fielding's going to read me the riot act for wasting his time. I stayed in bed, hoping the pain would pass off, but it didn't. Now he's actually coming there's no sign of it. Typical!'

'It's his job,' Carlo said, moving into her line of vision. 'Even if the pain's gone now, something caused it.'

Quickly, Venetia lowered her lashes, turning her head away from the Italian as a slow flush of guilt covered her face. Potty had remarked on her father's lateness, but she, Venetia, hadn't given it a moment's thought. She'd been too busy lying in wait for Carlo, plotting how to get him to go with her to Natasha's party. She should have gone to his room to check, she castigated herself, instead of trying to attract a man who was plainly bored by what he called her infatuation, who had taunted her cruelly, as good as telling her that a man would have to be paid in hard currency before he could bring himself to be seen with her on his arm in a public place!

Thankfully, she heard the sounds of the doctor's arrival and hurried to meet him, grateful, at least, for the colour that was gradually returning to her father's face. And, over an hour later, with the elderly man safely tucked up in bed, she walked with the doctor to his car.

'Grumbling appendix,' he told her, opening the door of the sturdy Volvo, putting his bag on the passenger seat. He had kind eyes in a weary face and he glanced up at Carlo, who had followed them out, 'Nothing to panic about, but call me if the pains recur. And liquids only for twenty-four hours. He should be fine in a couple of days.'

'I'll go up to him,' Venetia stated as the Volvo left, her voice stiff. She couldn't bear to look at Carlo. She would burst into noisy sobs if she did, remember just how cruel he had been, how he'd reduced what she felt for him to the level of juvenile infatuation, remember that by this time tomorrow he would be gone, and she would never see him again. Already her whole body was starting to shake.

'No.' His hand on her shoulder stopped her in her tracks, and she froze and closed her eyes, afraid that he would see the pain, the humiliation, the sheer blinding power of her love for him in the revealing depths. 'He was already falling asleep when I left him,' he stated. 'He had a restless night; a peaceful few hours will do him more good than anything. Besides——' he had two hands on her shoulders now, turning her round to face him '—Potty has promised to look in from time to time, to keep an eye on him.'

He was so close to her now. So close. She could feel the warmth of his body, the nearness of him, the indefinable, exquisitely potent force field of his masculinity as it reached out, as always, to enthral her, hold her spellbound.

Her lips began to tremble. Why couldn't he feel it too? Why did the only man she could ever love feel nothing for her except exasperation? She couldn't stay here with him a moment longer; it was too much to bear! Venetia felt the build-up of a sob inside her and tried to contain it, pushing at his body with her fists as the shameful tears welled up in her eyes, spilled over.

And he saw them, of course he did. He didn't miss a trick. And he would begin to taunt her again, call her a child; she knew he would, she thought hysterically, trying to hold her body rigid to counteract the weak trembling that was such a give-away.

But there was no cruelty in his husky voice as he pulled her into his arms.

'Ssh,' he whispered, dipping his dark head so that his cheek lay on hers. 'Don't cry. It's been a worrying couple of hours for you, but it's over now. Your father's going to be fine. You're suffering from reaction, that's all.'

All? Her sobs began in earnest as he held her, allowing her to cry all over his shirt, his hands gentling her as she clung to him, sliding rhythmically from her shoulders to her waist and back again. The way he was holding her, their bodies so close they might be one being, would have been sheer ecstasy if she hadn't already known he thought of her as a silly child, with as much sense in her head, as much capacity for real emotion, as a gaudy butterfly. The knowledge that he was leaving tomorrow was breaking her heart.

Gulping back a renewed spasm of sobbing, she tightened her arms around him, as if the sheer force of her love could keep him with her, now and for always. And felt his hands grow still against her back, felt the hard warmth of his palms burn through the thin fabric of her loose, sleeveless top, felt, beneath the pressure of her lush breasts and hips, the sudden rigidity of his lean masculine body.

And knew he was about to draw away, that he had been comforting her as he would have comforted an upset child, but, in the moment of her sexual initiative, the instinctive movements of her body against his, the way she had tried to use the power of her love for him to hold him, she had reminded him of her sexuality.

She wouldn't let him push her away, withdraw again behind that wall. She couldn't let him. She had broken through that wall. She had! He could no longer pretend she was a tiresome, overgrown child! Never more would he push her away!

But he did. Did it with a stark suddenness that left her reeling, searching his suddenly tight features with hurt, uncomprehending eyes.

Desperately her hands reached for him, but he took them in the iron-hard grip of one of his own, stepping back, holding her at a distance she felt as an aching void, making her throat tighten with anguish. And her huge, translucent eyes brimmed with unshed tears as she protested chokily, 'Don't push me away.'

'Just thank your lucky stars I have some self-control,' he came back tautly, his black eyes burning into hers with a ferocity she had never encountered before. 'If you were five years older, things might be different.' His magnificent eyes hardened to chips of jet, his browline a frowning black bar as he told her tightly, 'But you're just a child.'

'I'm not,' she cried wildly, twisting her hands within his iron grip. If she could only touch him again, tenderly yet with all the passion she now knew she was capable of, he would know she was all woman. She would show him that much. But his grip was cruel, ungiving, and she blurted frantically, her pride in tatters, 'I love you, Carlo! Don't leave me. Please don't leave me!' And heard him draw a rough breath deep into his lungs, his voice all ragged edges as he bit back ferociously,

'You tempt me too much! Do you know what you're doing to me? Do you?' He gave her a long black stare, his mouth tight, then dropped her hands as if her touch disgusted him, and walked rapidly back towards the house, taking her poor bruised heart with him.

Venetia woke feeling smothered, anxious to the point of panic, not knowing the cause.

Agitatedly she pushed at the bedcovers, flinging them off the bed, till they lay in a slithery scarlet satin pool on the thick white carpet, and gazed around her with wide, bewildered eyes.

Then the feeling of being in a waking nightmare subsided as she pin-pointed the source of her anxiety. It wasn't her father, that was for sure. Oh, she was still concerned after yesterday's fright, but nothing more than that. As long as he kept to a liquid-only diet today and took a few days off work, there was every reason to expect that the grumbling appendix would behave itself.

The root of her misery lay with her beloved Carlo. She drew her knees up to her chin and wrapped her arms around them, her long black hair all over the place. Despite her protestations of love, the way she'd pleaded with him to stay—she went hot with shame when she recalled her impassioned outburst—he had every intention of leaving, setting out for the airport in his hired car at noon.

After he'd walked away from her, back to the house, she had felt more alone and miserable than ever before in her young life. She hadn't known how to handle the sensation of utter despair, especially when, a few minutes later, she'd seen him shoot off down the drive in the hired Fiesta.

In between checking on her father, she'd hung around waiting for Carlo to return, restlessly pacing the terrace, trying to work out what she should say to him when she saw him next. She'd felt physically and mentally shattered by what had happened, by the way she'd behaved.

But the hours had stretched into a day that had seemed endless. No sign of him. And she hadn't been able to touch the salad Potty had given her for lunch, or the delicious grilled trout that had been produced at dinner.

'He's certainly making sure he sees plenty of the area before he leaves tomorrow,' Potty had remarked drily as she'd removed the plate of fish Venetia had mangled with her fork, her shrewd eyes on the unused place-setting on the opposite side of the table, the empty chair.

Venetia had dredged up a pale smile, the small, defeated shrug of her shoulder telling all there was to tell, and Potty had said, her voice gruff, 'Don't take on so. He's not the only pebble on the beach.'

Watching the housekeeper trundle out of the room, Venetia had cursed herself for being so transparent. She had laid herself open to Potty's platitudes and Carlo's scorn. He had known what she felt, even before she had told him she loved him, and had reduced it to the level of mere infatuation.

And Potty was wrong. As far as she was concerned he was the only man she would ever love with this level of passionate intensity. But it wasn't any use, she thought miserably; he had made that very plain. So she was simply going to have to come to terms with it, somehow, and try to decide how she would react when she saw him next, what she would say.

But she needn't have agonised so deeply because her confidence had taken the final annihilating blow when, while she'd been playing Scrabble with her father late last evening, Carlo had at last put in an appearance.

He hadn't looked at her; she might not have been in the room as he'd made suitably concerned enquiries about the state of her father's health.

And her face had turned pale when he'd gone on to say, 'If you're sure you're on the mend, I'll take my flight to Rome tomorrow, as arranged. But if you've the slightest doubt and would like me to stay on, I can cancel it.'

And Venetia had held her breath, willing her father to ask Carlo to stay. But he didn't. Of course he didn't.

'I'm fine,' the older man had stated. 'Once I've survived the starvation diet I'll be better than new! And I've asked Carew to drop by first thing in the morning. I'll brief him to cover my absence for the next couple of days. So don't alter your plans because I had a stomach-ache—there's absolutely no need.'

'If you're sure...'

A flicker of something—relief?—had moved across the hard profile, then the sensual mouth had firmed as he'd added, 'After a great deal of thought, I've reached a decision of some importance, and I'd like to discuss it with you. Tomorrow morning—after you've seen Carew?'

'Why not now?' The older man gestured to the armchair on the other side of his big old-fashioned bed, his smile expansive. 'And pour yourself a Scotch, why don't you? The decanter's on top of the dressing-chest.'

Involuntarily, or so it seemed to Venetia, the black eyes were at last turned in her direction. And almost immediately back to her father, the slightly accented, fascinating voice uncompromising as he insisted, 'Tomorrow would be better.'

So he had reached some decision, to do with business—what else?—and refused to discuss it in front of her, Venetia had thought on a spasm of stinging pain. He wouldn't discuss anything of importance while she was around. He thought she was a bird-brain.

She had kept her eyes on her clenched hands during the short silence that had preceded his exit and had gone to bed herself soon after, every last bone in her body weakened by the myriad hurts he was so good at inflicting—intentionally or otherwise.

And this morning she felt no better, she decided hollowly as she pushed the hair back from her face and gazed blearily around her room. Twelve months ago she'd insisted on having it redecorated to her own specifications, sweeping away the girlish frills and flower-speckled wallpaper, the pink and fawn carpet and flounced pink curtains. Now the furniture was matt black and, apart from the white carpet, everything else was scarlet.

She had been thrilled with it, she remembered, revelling in the sensuous velvets and satin. Now, looking around her at the beginning of what promised to be another hot summer day, she knew it was tacky, and a part of her looked back and mourned the passing of her ebullient self, the wonderful adventure of her emergence from childhood, all that fantastic self-confidence that had been so ruthlessly destroyed when she'd fallen in love with the unattainable.

When she finally got out of bed and went to stand under the shower, she found she was shaking. Carlo was leaving today and they weren't likely to meet again. Her father and Simon were more than capable of running the business he had shares in; it had ticked over for years without the Rossi family doing any more than pocket the dividends. Besides, he was running the diverse Rossi business empire virtually single-handedly now that his father had opted to take a back seat because of failing health. It wasn't likely he'd visit England again in a hurry.

Covering her dripping, voluptuous nakedness with a bath-sheet, she wondered forlornly if he would ever spare her a passing thought, and decided he wouldn't. The flock of lovely, elegant ladies whose undoubted existence Potty had guessed at would ensure that she, Venetia, the overgrown schoolgirl whose protestations of love must have embarrassed him so, would be pretty promptly erased from his memory.

Indifferent now to how she looked, she pulled on a pair of shabby cotton jeans and the only school blouse that hadn't been cut up for polishing rags, then mooched along to see her father.

Potty had taken him a jug of freshly squeezed orange juice, and his bed was covered with papers and files.

'Should you be working?' she asked concernedly, twisting her long, shiny hair back behind her head, wishing she'd taken the time to plait it, because today was going to be boiling.

'I'm not,' he told her, staring at her over the top of his glasses. 'Just getting things in some sort of coherent order to pass on to Simon when he arrives. Which should be any time now. Would you like to ask him to stay to lunch, to keep you company?'

There was only one man's company she wanted. Trouble was, he didn't want hers. She shook her head mutely and her father frowned.

'What's wrong? You look drained. You're not still worried about me? Because if you are—don't.'

'It's the heat,' she lied, wondering if she would ever feel happy again, fully alive and carefree. She couldn't imagine it, somehow.

'Then go and cool off in the pool, poppet. Simon can find his own way up and Carlo's busy in the library—dictating reports, he said. So you can have a nice, relaxing morning all to yourself.'

Returning to her room, she decided that her father's idea wasn't a bad one at that. She wasn't going to make a fool of herself a second time. She'd keep right out of Carlo's way; there was no point in trying to make her peace with him. When Simon had been and gone Carlo would have his business discussion with her father and take off to the airport. Until then she would make herself scarce. The pool in the old walled courtyard would be as good a place as any to hide out.

Her old school regulation swimsuit was now too tight in various places, and the bikinis she'd lashed out on to replace it were, on consideration, barely decent. Shrugging her square shoulders, she decided it didn't matter. No one would see her and she'd use a towelling robe to cover up as she walked through the house.

The water was deliciously cool, and a few punishing lengths of the pool left her feeling more relaxed as she finally turned over and floated idly on her back. If she didn't think, if she simply concentrated on staying afloat, then she might be able to stay calm enough to say goodbye to Carlo in an hour or two, with some composure, at least.

The knife-thrust of pain at the very idea of having to say goodbye to him at all made her clench her teeth, made her knees jerk up to her chest in a purely reflex action, sending her down to the blue tiles six feet below. And she didn't care if she never surfaced, but she bobbed up to the top, shaking the water out of her eyes, and saw Simon silhouetted against the sun, and wished herself down at the bottom again because she didn't want to have to talk to anyone. She was too depressed.

'That looks good.' He sounded amused, breathless, too, as if he'd been running. 'If someone would lend me a pair of briefs, I'd join you. Unless——' his voice thickened '—you'd like to see me in the nude?'

'Why on earth should I want to do that?' she retorted crossly, diving for the steps and hauling herself up, because she had to get out of here. He had spoiled what little pleasure there'd been in the morning.

Frowning, she planted her feet on the tiled surround. On the last two occasions they'd been out together Simon had been far too pushy, his language at times too coarse for her liking. She had put up with it only because the only other option had been to stay home, miss out on all the fun, hardly ever see her friends.

In future she'd happily stay at home until such time as her father could be persuaded she would be safe without an escort of his choosing—and Simon could go find someone else to try to paw around. She was tired of having to slap him down.

And when she saw the way he was looking at her she wished she'd stayed in the water. The bikini left hardly anything at all to the imagination, the droplets of water on her creamy skin emphasising the lush curves.

Venetia made a grab for her robe, but he got there first, holding it behind his back with one hand.

'Don't spoil the fun,' he said thickly. 'I want to see the goods on display.'

She had never realised just what a lewd creep he was, she thought furiously, gritting her teeth.

The first few times they'd been out together he'd been everything she had expected a hand-picked escort to be—considerate, amusing and protective. But lately he had made his sexual interest blatantly known, and their outings had grown progressively more like a wrestling match than the pleasant evenings they were meant to be.

Her father would blow a fuse if he had the slightest inkling of the way things were. And she shouted crossly, 'Does my father know you're here? Does he have any idea what you're up to?'

'Oh, come on!' he responded peevishly. 'I've already seen him and taken my orders like a good little employee. What's wrong with our having a little fun? Besides, he's got the big-shot Signor Rossi with him right now—that should keep him fully occupied.' His eyes went hot as they raked the exposed curves she was beginning to wish she hadn't got. 'You know how I feel about you, and don't try to pretend you're not ripe and ready for it!'

Venetia forgot all about her semi-nakedness as she faced him down with icy fury, her sparking eyes daring him to come one step nearer as she snapped, 'You disgust me! And if I didn't find you totally beneath contempt, beneath notice, I'd get my father to fire you on the spot!'

She turned quickly, intent only on getting away from his hateful presence, his lustful eyes and crude taunts, not wary enough to prevent him lunging forward, grabbing the back of her bikini top.

The flimsy strap broke at once and her stride faltered as she grabbed at the tiny triangles of fabric, trying to retain a modicum of decency, and then he was manhandling her, hauling her round, catching her off balance as he growled into her ear, 'By the time I've finished with you, shown you what it's all about, the last thing you'll be thinking about is getting me fired, I promise!'

He was too strong for her, thinking on his feet as he sank on to one of the loungers, pulling her down on top of him, the breath knocked out of her lungs with the suddenness of it all as she found herself lying on top of him on her back, one of his hands splayed out on the curve of her stomach, the other clutching one of her naked breasts.

The shock of what had happened, the disgust, made her body go rigid, her long legs splayed out in seeming wanton abandon as she fought to gather her strength, gather enough to get herself out of this hatefully degrading situation. And, dragging a deep breath through her lungs, shuddering as she felt his hand tighten on her breast, she heard, through the red mist of rage behind her closed eyes, the hard and derisive tones of Carlo Rossi.

'I won't apologise for intruding. In fact, I'm glad I did.' And, as her eyes winged open in absolute horror, before she could even begin to exonerate herself she heard him say, his deep voice iced with sarcasm, 'Don't bother to get up, children. I can see myself off.'

And then, again, and very finally, she watched him walk away.

CHAPTER THREE

'DID you know he was going to be at the funeral?' Venetia asked as she and Simon settled in the back seat of the limousine and the uniformed driver swept sedately away from the church. 'I hope he doesn't imagine he can come back to the house.'

Simon shrugged. 'I didn't know he'd be here, but I half expected it. After all, you will have inherited your father's shares in Ross UK, and as he owns the remaining block he'll want to watch over his interests.'

She gave him a bleak sideways look, the black veiling on the tiny pillbox hat disguising the redness of her eyes. Now wasn't the time to talk of business, of Carlo Rossi's interests in the struggling company. It was bad enough that he was here.

She sighed, lacing her black-gloved fingers together in her lap. Today had been ordeal enough without looking across her beloved father's open grave to encounter the hard black stare of the man she had once believed she would love forever, the man she would have given her life for if she'd been called upon to do so.

'Keep your pecker up.' Simon touched her clenched hands briefly with his. 'We'll get rid of everyone as soon as we decently can and you can have a peaceful afternoon. I'll stay and keep you company and we'll have a quiet dinner together. I don't want you to be left on your own.'

She nodded, suddenly too choked to speak. The death of her father a week ago had been a terrible shock. He hadn't told anyone of his heart condition, and when he'd suffered a massive coronary, died in his sleep, she hadn't been able to believe it. In a way, she still couldn't. She didn't know how she would have managed, coped with the arrangements, without Simon. During the last seven days she seemed to have reverted to the level of an inexperienced, frightened child, the woman she'd so painstakingly schooled herself to become over the last six years obliterated by the trauma, the grief of losing her father.

But she was back in control again now, she assured herself as the car drew up in front of the house. She had to be. Her chin lifted imperiously below the veil as she readied herself to go into the house to receive the other mourners.

Potty had attended the funeral, of course—she was like one of the family—and had organised the firm of caterers who would now be putting the final touches to the cold buffet.

Carlo wouldn't be crass enough to appear, she told herself, stumbling a little as the mere thought of him made her legs go weak.

'You OK?' Simon placed a solicitous hand beneath her elbow and she leaned against him gratefully for a moment, hearing expensive clunks as other cars parked on the drive behind them.

'Yes, of course,' she told him, dragging herself together. She didn't need to be a genius to know exactly why the mere thought of Carlo Rossi affected her this way. Sheer, excruciating embarrassment.

Six years ago, during a fateful week one summer, she had thrown herself at his head. And the last time he'd seen her she had been sprawled out all over Simon, naked apart from a seriously small bikini bottom.

Colour flared briefly over her face as she recalled that occasion. She had thought she would die from the pain of his going, the embarrassment of the situation, her rage at Simon for being the cause of this final, degrading humiliation.

Strangely enough, over the years she had grown fond of Simon. As if the other man's arrival on the scene all those years ago had brought him back to his senses, he hadn't been able to apologise profusely enough. The next day he had sent her flowers, but he hadn't tried to see her or speak to her.

It had been the following Christmas, when her father had invited him to the house for drinks, before she'd as much as set eyes on him again. He had been charming, but not pushy, his grey eyes still abjectly apologetic whenever they caught hers.

And then, of course, after two years of intense secretarial and business training, she had joined her father's firm, and it had been Simon who had helped her up through the various levels of management, his knowledge and patience, allied to her determination to excel, carrying her right to the top.

So much so that when, nearly a year ago, her father had gone into semi-retirement—not telling them his health was in a precarious state, but that, at his age, he felt he had earned some leisure time—he had had no hesitation in allowing her to take over the reins he had held so firmly in his own hands.

She knew he had been proud of her and if he had wondered why his frivolous, party-loving, spendthrift offspring had changed overnight into a workaholic, he had never asked. In those weeks and months since Carlo had left she hadn't cared much about anything. Deciding to make a career in her father's company had made sense simply because it made him happy.

Tears stung the backs of her eyes and she blinked them away. No point in looking back; she had taught herself that much. Resolutely she walked into the house, her back ramrod-straight beneath the sombre black fabric of her slim-fitting suit, her smile reserved as she received the condolences of the mourners, grateful for Simon's presence at her side.

Murmuring suitable responses, her face aching with the effort of keeping the pasted smile in place, she glanced past the shoulders of the solemn-faced representative of the Newcastle retail outlet to the panelled hall beyond and went icily cold as a pain as searing as a knife-thrust turned her face parchment-white.

Carlo! She should have expected this and mentally prepared herself, instead of sticking her head in the sand like an ostrich, pretending he wouldn't muscle in where he wasn't invited—or welcome.

Six years hadn't changed him, except to score the character lines a little more deeply on his arrogantly masculine features, his body as perfectly honed as ever, his air of authority perhaps more boldly stamped. Already more than a few female heads were turned in his direction, fascinated by such a blindingly charismatic specimen of the male of the species.

Unable to help herself, Venetia shuddered right down to the soles of her high-heeled shoes. And Simon said to the latest group to wander up to pay their respects, 'I think Venetia could stand a drink. Do please excuse us for a moment.' Adding as he gently drew her aside, 'You look awful. Are you going to faint?'

He looked as if he wouldn't know what to do if she replied in the affirmative, and that raised a ghost of a genuine smile as she put his mind at rest and told him, 'I've never fainted in my life. But you're right, I could use a drink. Trying to find something to say to all these people is proving more of an ordeal than I ever imagined.'

Not for the world would she reveal how shattered she was by Carlo's reappearance on the scene, how the memory of the way he'd looked at her as she lay sprawled all over Simon could still turn her sick with shame and embarrassment. If she said anything of the kind it would bring that day right back again, as vivid and painful as ever, disturbing the status quo.

Simon had done all the apologising necessary, promising that such a thing would never happen again. And it certainly hadn't, and he'd been so patient and helpful while she'd been learning the ropes, so supportive when her father had eventually handed the reins over to her, and she didn't know how on earth she would have coped without him during this last week. She had long since forgiven him because, no matter how unwelcome his attentions had been, he hadn't ruined things for her with Carlo. Carlo hadn't been interested; for him she'd been a pain in the neck and, looking back, she could see why.

'Drink this.' He put a glass of brandy in her hands, closing his fingers over hers as they tightened round the bowl. 'And don't look so worried; people are already getting ready to leave. You can soon put your feet up and relax, and in the meantime I'll do the rounds if you like, and thank everyone for coming.'

'It's OK, I'll be fine,' she murmured, lifting the glass to her lips. But she was grateful for his offer, all the same. She was glad she'd been able to learn to like and trust him all over again, she decided, closing her eyes just for a second as the smooth, expensive brandy slid down her throat, warming and strengthening her.

And when she opened them again she was looking directly into a pair of hostile black eyes, and she caught her breath, feeling her insides turn over sickly as the fascinating voice flooded her with the pain of memories she had mistakenly believed long forgotten.

'My sincere condolences on your loss, Venetia. Your father was a fine man and I know how deeply you cared for each other.'

'Thank you.' The words emerged stiffly, her tongue feeling like a lump of wood although her lips were quivering. She had never expected to have to see him again, which had been pretty stupid of her, she now realised, considering that he owned a large block of shares—a minority only by a whisker—in her father's company. Her company now, she recognised hollowly, as he acknowledged,

'Carew. Still making yourself useful, I see. Your wife not with you?'

To her intense annoyance, Venetia felt her face go hot. The stress he'd laid on the word 'useful', the cynical curl of his mouth as his hooded eyes had rested on the supportive hand Simon had placed around her waist, had been forcibly and cruelly meant to let her know he had total recall of the last occasion he'd seen them together.

And how the hell did he know Simon was married? Had he been checking up on them? There had been occasional phone calls between him and her father; he must have gathered the news that way. And Simon was mumbling, 'Angie couldn't be here, I'm afraid. She's away on an assignment.'

He had gone brick-red, too, Venetia noted crossly. The way they had both flushed must make them look as if they had something to be guilty about. She had to pull herself together. Carlo meant less than nothing to her now and it was time she started to behave like the adult woman she was instead of acting like a terrified schoolgirl in front of a stern headmaster. Besides, she knew why Simon looked so uneasy. He and Angie had only been married for six months, and already the way her modelling career kept them so much apart was beginning to cause furious quarrels. Angie had no intention of becoming a conventional wife, supporting her husband's career, while she had her own to consider.

An eloquent shrug of impeccably suited shoulders, an ironic curl of the beautiful mouth told her he didn't set much store by mumbled excuses. Actions, for him, spoke louder than words.

As if Simon had picked that up, too, his hand slid away from her slender waist, and Carlo's eyes made a slow assessment of her, from the top of her tiny hat to the tips of her expensively shod toes.

'Physically, you've changed.' It was neither a regret nor a compliment, simply a statement of fact which she acknowledged with a slight, indifferent nod of her head. The lushness which had been a hallmark of her late teens had gone, replaced by a slenderness that owed everything to the fact that she watched what she ate. And the long waterfall of jet hair had been cropped to a sleek, jaw-length bob.

There was nothing she could say to that remark without calling back that long-ago week when she had behaved so stupidly. She wished he would leave, go back to Rome, or wherever, and, as if her words might magic him away, or at least let him understand exactly how unwelcome she found his presence, she told him coolly, 'It was good of you to make time in your busy life to come over for today. Father would have appreciated it.' She put down the glass she'd forgotten she'd been holding, sliding in the *coup de grâce*. 'I hope you have a comfortable journey back. Don't let us keep you.'

Which earned her the hint of an acknowledging smile, an unspoken *touché*, and she turned with relief as Potty approached, the white apron she wore over her simple black dress informing everyone she was back on duty again.

'Some of your guests are on the point of leaving, pet. I thought you ought to know. And if you don't want me for anything at the moment, I'll get Mr Carew's room ready, if that's all right.'

Venetia frowned, her translucent eyes seeking Simon. She'd acquiesced when he'd suggested keeping her company for dinner this evening, but this was the first she'd heard about him staying overnight. Mentally shrugging, she decided he'd literally meant what he'd said when he'd told her he didn't want her to be alone tonight. That Potty would be here would mean nothing to him because as far as he was concerned the housekeeper was a servant and, as such, didn't count.

'I don't think you should be left alone, not tonight,' Simon confirmed her guesswork. 'I spoke to Mrs Potts about it earlier,' he added stiltedly, not looking at anyone.

Venetia sighed. It made no difference to her whether he stayed overnight or not, and she supposed he thought he was being kind, looking after her as he knew her father would have wanted him to. But she would have liked to be consulted. And then she went cold with shocked disbelief as Carlo's voice slid urbanely between them.

'I agree with you, Carew. However, as I shall be here for a few days, there won't be any need for you to stay.'

As he turned to the housekeeper the first hint of warmth he had displayed since his arrival softened the black hostility of his eyes and curved the long, sculpted mouth. 'I'll use the room you would have given Carew, but don't bother making up the bed; I can do that myself.'

'You could just as easily book yourself into a hotel, too!' The hot words were out before Venetia could stop them, and the sting she'd heard in her voice left her feeling shaken. She didn't want him here, a grim reminder of her shameful behaviour all those years ago, but did she have to lose her poise to this extent, letting him think he could still affect her when, in reality, he didn't?

Instinctively, she edged closer to Simon, caught the cynical shaft of light in Carlo's midnight eyes and looked quickly away, grinding her teeth with annoyance as she heard the smooth flattery of his sexy voice as he turned her suggestion down flat.

'Why a hotel, when I can stay here? Believe me, Potty's cooking is a cherished memory of mine, the best of the memories I took back to Italy with me six years ago.'

And no prizes for guessing which would have been the worst, Venetia thought, embarrassment making her feel distinctly queasy as she watched Potty go pink and begin to bridle at the compliment as she answered, 'Make up your own bed? What nonsense! It will be my pleasure. I'll give you the room you had last time—you said you liked the view of the garden, remember? We'll enjoy having you here again.'

Speak for yourself, Venetia thought acidly as the housekeeper waddled away, then quickly followed her, not looking at either of the two men. They could sort out between them whether they would both be staying overnight. She, obviously, was to be allowed no say in the matter!

Saying goodbye to the people who had been invited back to the house after her father's funeral, thanking them for coming, for showing their respect and giving her their support took longer than she had expected, and she was longing to be alone, to have the time and the space to come to terms with her loss, when the last guest straggled out.

It was Simon, and she had to blink, to look at him twice, before she realised who he was. And she allowed the painful smile she had pasted on to her face to slip as he said drearily, 'He Who Must Be Obeyed has given me my marching orders. He says he'll speak to me tomorrow, and the day after that he's going to call a management meeting. It appears he wants you all to himself for the rest of the day. But don't let him wear you out with non-stop business discussions. You already look exhausted.'

'Thanks for boosting my ego, Si,' she responded drily, mentally stiffening her spine. Business discussions she could handle—just. But if he started to taunt her with reminders of just how shamelessly she had behaved all those years ago she would kill him! 'Where is he now?' she added quietly, suppressing the ridiculous fear that he was lurking somewhere in the shadows, waiting to pounce, rubbing his hands in anticipation of tormenting her with the memories of how she had thrown herself at his head, telling him she loved him while all the time, apparently, doing the same thing to Simon!

The big hall was empty; so was the reception-room, except for the caterers who were dismantling the buffet, and Simon said, a sneer in his voice, 'The last time I saw him, your housekeeper was dragging him away to the kitchen for "A nice cup of tea and a slice of my fruit cake—proper cake, not like the stuff those catering firms come up with". I think the woman's going senile. She won't find it easy to land another cushy number when you sell up here. You have thought about my suggestion, haven't you?'

Walking to the door with him, Venetia frowned. Right now she didn't feel up to discussing the possible sale of this house. The grief she felt for the loss of her father was too new, too raw. Parting with the house she had lived in all her life would be a wrenching decision she knew she wasn't fit to deal impartially with right now.

And Simon seemed to understand because, with his hand on the door now, he turned and faced her, his features softening as he told her, 'Forget I even mentioned it. We'll get together and discuss the ramifications when you're feeling less fraught. I don't want to push you into a decision you're not ready to make; I'm too fond of you to do that. But if I'd stayed with you tonight, as I'd planned, we could have had a nice relaxed chat—there's something important I want to talk to you about, in any case.'

His voice had taken on a peevish note, and Venetia reached past him to open the door, shivering suddenly in the cold early March air.

It was almost dark now; the short late winter day had gone quickly, which was a blessing because the sooner it was over the sooner she would be able to come to terms with the aching sadness of losing the father who had been so dear to her.

And whatever Simon had to say, no matter how 'important', she didn't want to hear it, not yet. And, despite what he'd said about not wanting to push her into a decision over the sale of this house, she suspected that he'd been aiming to do just that, and her suspicions were confirmed when he closed the door again and said tightly, 'Look, if you want me to stay, I will—never mind what Rossi says. It's your home, after all; he can't tell me to leave—he hasn't got the right. You just tell him you want me here, and he can shove off if he doesn't like it. Then we can have a nice lazy evening and talk like the old friends we are.'

Just for a second, Venetia was tempted. She would like nothing better than to show the Italian that he couldn't throw his weight around, arbitrarily decide who did—and who did not—stay overnight in her own home! But the thought of the hassle, of long hours of Simon's undiluted company, of the cosy chat he had talked about, when he would no doubt insist that this house had to go, was something she was too mentally exhausted to contemplate.

'I don't think so,' she dismissed firmly; then, as his lower lip jutted petulantly, she hurried to soften her refusal to do as he'd suggested because, after all, he'd only been thinking of her best interests. 'I'm not up to anything much at the moment.' She smiled gently, placing a slender hand on his arm. 'Not even chatting to old friends. When the caterers have left I'll probably have a bath and go straight to my room. Signor Rossi will have to entertain himself.' Because she darned well wasn't going to. She'd have to feel a whole lot stronger, right back in control, before she could stomach the embarrassment of having to face him on a one-to-one basis.

'If that's what you want.' Simon looked mollified. 'I'll phone you and fix up a quiet evening, just the two of us. Angie's going to be away for at least another week. And in the meantime don't let Rossi give you any hassle as far as the business is concerned—or anything else, for that matter.'

'I won't,' she promised, suddenly longing for him to go, the relief when he opened the door again making her accept the sudden kiss he dropped on her lips.

The instinct to rub her mouth as she watched him walk towards his parked car was not only insulting but childish, she recognised, resisting it, lifting a hand in answer to his farewell salute as he opened the car door. In all the time she'd worked so closely with him he had never tried to touch her, and his kiss had been nothing more than a friendly gesture of support at this sad time, nothing to get in a stew about, no need to start shuddering inside, to allow memories of how he had once behaved to creep in and spoil the friendly relationship they now had. Six years ago he had been young and full of himself, convinced he was God's gift. He was older and wiser and kinder now.

She stepped back into the hall, closing the door, wondering how long the caterers would be, and from behind her the deep, slightly accented voice said witheringly, 'Very touching. Gone home to nurse his frustration, has he? Does his wife know you were planning to spend the night together?'

'Hardly!' She swung round on one spindly heel, her face running with immediate, wrathful colour. How dared he make such an assumption? How dared he? But, apart from the angry flush, she held herself under some kind of control, putting a cool sneer in her voice as she questioned, 'Do you tell your wife every time you play away from home?'

'As I don't have one, the question doesn't arise,' he responded, his dark eyes revealing the extent of his disgust.

But Venetia didn't flinch; she held his disparaging gaze, her chin up, her eyes, witch-like and slanting, sometimes so pale that they looked like crystal, but now darkening to cold violet. Six years ago he had left this house, taking with him the worst possible impression of her, and on his return he had brought his miserable conceptions back with him, prepared to believe the very worst of her, turning an old friend's offer to keep her company on this sad night into a sordid intrigue, the affectionate kiss he had obviously witnessed adding fuel to the evil flames of his sick imagination!

The adrenalin running well now, she stared fixedly up at his austere, cold features. He could think what he liked—she simply didn't care; and if he really wanted to believe the worst of her she'd give him some help!

Trying to ignore the way her knees were shaking—with outrage and fury, she guessed—she sauntered towards him, slanting a mocking glance in his direction as she drew level, her eyes glinting wickedly behind the tiny black veil as she affected a small, cat-like yawn, delicately tapping her teeth with the tips of her fingernails before drawling, 'Believe it or not, I can stand to spend the occasional night alone. And don't worry——' she glided away, heading for the stairs, lobbing back at him, almost beginning to enjoy herself '—you're quite safe. These days I only play with married men—that way I get all the fun and none of the drudgery.'

CHAPTER FOUR

AS SOON as Venetia closed the bedroom door behind her she felt deeply ashamed of herself—a cold, racking shame that had her rooted to the spot, her arms wrapped tightly around her shivering body.

What on earth had possessed her to say such things, to act that way? Carlo Rossi meant less than nothing to her now. She had barely spared him a thought in years. So why should one look from those black, hostile eyes have her reacting as if she were a heartless, promiscuous tramp? And on the day of her beloved father's funeral, too! That alone was enough to make her feel more than doubly degraded.

Tears welled in her eyes, but she blinked them ferociously away, dragged in a shuddering breath, and straightened her shoulders. And behind her she heard a rap on the heavy polished wood of the door, heard Potty calling her name.

'Come on in,' she answered automatically, her movements rigid as she walked over to the dressing-table to remove her hat. She would never want to see it, or the neat, structured black suit again. She didn't want anything to remind her of this dreadful day.

'I wondered where you'd got to.' There was a hint of reproof in the housekeeper's voice, but Venetia ignored it, meeting her own reflected eyes in the glass. They looked far too big for her face, the pallor of which was heightened by the sleek black jaw-length fall of her hair. 'The caterers have gone and I thought you and Signor

Rossi might prefer an early dinner. Just one of my casseroles, nothing elaborate. It's going to be a raw night, so I'll serve it in the breakfast-room; it's nice and cosy there.'

Venetia shrugged, already unbuttoning the jacket of her suit. Carlo could have his dinner from a dustbin lid in the back yard for all she cared. And she said tonelessly, 'I don't want anything. I'm not hungry. I'll have a bath and an early night.'

'You'd have eaten if that Simon had stayed, as he wanted to,' Potty pointed out scathingly. 'You're doing yourself no good at all!' And she left, banging the door behind her, relieving her tension.

Venetia clamped her lips together firmly, refusing to think about what Potty had said. She wasn't going to think about anything, not tonight. If she did, she might well break down completely.

Tomorrow would be soon enough to try and work things out. She would phone Simon, she decided, arrange a meeting and talk everything through with him. He would give her impartial advice.

That much decided on, she made her mind a blank and continued undressing, folding the suit carefully and putting it neatly away in the bottom of her wardrobe, the veiled hat on top. She would donate them to a charity shop, maybe tomorrow.

And half an hour later she emerged from the adjoining bathroom, rubbing her hair with a towel, her tall slenderness emphasised by the thirties-style white satin nightdress she wore. Tossing the towel on to a chair, she dragged a comb through her hair and walked over to twitch the curtains aside, trying to contain the snarling inner restlessness that had come out of nowhere.

It was pitch-black, of course, only the pinpricks of light from distant farmhouses and cottages to remind her that she was on an inhabited planet. No stars at all, so the cloud layer must be thick. Snow had been forecast; she had heard someone at the funeral saying as much, remarking that it was lucky it had held off so far...

But she wasn't going to think about the funeral.

She walked quickly to the bookshelves on one side of the bed and selected a luridly jacketed sex-and-shopping saga. She had bought it out of curiosity, having heard that it had earned its author a million-dollar advance, but had never been able to finish it.

Tonight it could well answer the question of how she could get to sleep without lying awake for hours grieving, anxiously worrying over the best way to handle the future. She would read every word even if it bored her stupid, focus her mind on the *risqué* goings-on between the covers, blocking out everything else until, eventually, sheer boredom sent her to sleep.

As she slipped beneath the duvet in its slate-grey cover, her mind winged back betrayingly to that night over six years ago. The night Carlo had left. She had thrown herself on to the scarlet satin bedspread, clawing the rich fabric with her hands, weeping her heart out... And two months later she had altered to such an extent that she had, on a reflex of distaste, thrown out the matt black furniture, the scarlet satins and velvets. It was tacky and tasteless, and it had reminded her of the voluptuous side of her character she had clinically decided to starve out of existence...

Gritting her teeth, she wrenched her wayward mind away from such backward-looking, miry tracks, stacked the white-cotton-covered pillows behind her, and opened her book. It was going to be a long night...

And she had barely reached the end of the first chapter when a brisk rapping on the door had her tossing the book aside with relief, its cover a splash of garish colour on the sober-toned duvet.

Potty again, she decided resignedly, coming to nag her about not eating dinner. She would apologise for her earlier brusqueness, she thought on an uneasy pang of guilt. The elderly woman had been with them so long that she was almost part of the family and she, too, would be grieving, probably anxious about the future.

But it certainly wasn't the housekeeper who filled the door-frame. Carlo. And his mood wasn't too sweet, judging by the hard, clamping line of his mouth, the way he shot the door back in its frame with a snappy movement of one solid shoulder.

He was carrying a tray, and Venetia's chin went up, her body rigid with outrage and something she didn't want to try to put a name to. And she said heatedly, 'I don't remember inviting you to my room. Get out.' And wondered, too late, just what it was about him that provoked such a reaction. And regretted having shown, yet again, just how easily he could get her on the defensive. He meant nothing at all to her now—that was the image she should be projecting—so she tried for a tone of indifferent dismissal as she tacked on, 'If you've brought me something to eat, you can take it away. I don't want it. Sorry.'

She made to reach for her book, but his progress across the room had been unhesitating, despite her acid comments, and he put the tray down across her thighs, none too graciously, and ordered, 'Eat. Or I'll make you. And I don't think either one of us would find that a particularly elevating experience.'

Venetia frowned at the bowl of steaming soup and reluctantly rejected the course of outright disobedience. He had meant what he'd said when he'd threatened to force-feed her. Dipping the spoon into the bowl, she swirled it around, shooting him a stony glare as she told him, 'There's no need for you to stand over me,' and found the ironic curl of his mouth, the black, brooding intensity of his magnificent eyes too disturbing for her peace of mind, and couldn't stop the shiver that ran over her naked skin as he informed her drily,

'Potty tells me you haven't eaten enough to keep a fly alive just lately, so I'm staying to make sure you finish the last drop of that soup.'

Spoken like the despot he was, she thought mutinously, watching the way his black gaze drifted from the lurid book-jacket to her body, the white satin deeply cut at the neckline, leaving her arms naked, emphasising the creamy tones of her skin.

Her flesh went hot beneath the cynical, lazy drift of his eyes, and she knew that what he would see as her choice of reading matter and the seductive cut of the satin nightgown would reinforce the low opinion he had of her morals. Not that she had exactly helped to dispel that opinion, she groaned inwardly, spooning up some of the now cooling soup because the sooner she finished it, presumably, the sooner he would leave.

But he didn't help, just standing there. His powerful physique was lethal; the breadth of shoulder allied to the sheer animal grace of narrow hips and long, elegant limbs was making her throat close up, making it difficult to swallow the dratted soup. And why should he care, anyway, whether she ate or not?

He obviously thought she was beneath contempt—his opinion based on what had happened so long ago and her own idiotic comments this afternoon. He wouldn't care if she died of starvation in front of his eyes. So why should he be this determined to break the pattern of the last week when the shock of her father's death had ruined even the small appetite she had ruthlessly trained herself to have?

And that thought brought the end of her reluctant attempt to finish what was left in the bowl. Brought her loss keening back to her, ripping her soul. Despairingly, she thrust the tray away and brought her hands up to cover her face, the build-up of a sob beneath her breastbone like a pain that would rend her in two.

Grief, for Venetia, was a private thing, and she hadn't meant this to happen. That she should break down in front of the one man she had continually debased herself in front of six years ago was the final humiliation. But she could no more stop the tears from falling than she could magic him away by sheer will-power alone.

Through the storm of emotion she felt the mattress dip, his body nudging against hers as he gently but firmly dragged her hands away from her face, his dark, fathomless eyes oddly liquid as they searched her stricken features.

Venetia dragged her lower lip between her teeth, trying to smother the sob that was building up inside her chest and making her breasts push against the sleek white fabric, and felt her body go very still, as if it had been turned to stone, as the darkly brooding intensity of his eyes found the pale anguish of her own. And held. And she couldn't look away because she was drowning in those black, liquid depths, mesmerised by something that was stronger than her will.

'*Santa Maria*!' The sensual line of his expressive mouth hardened as his gaze fell from her tear-filled eyes, past the frenetically beating pulse at the base of her long, elegant neck to the thrusting breasts beneath the barely concealing slither of satin.

His eyes closed suddenly, the sternly handsome features formidable, and she caught her breath, sensing his utter withdrawal from the brink of something she couldn't name; she shuddered violently as he took the fragile perfection of her hands and twined them around his neck only an instant before gathering her into his arms and commanding thickly, 'Cry for your father. Do not hide your grief, Venetia. It is nothing to be ashamed of.'

And that released the floodgates, and for the second time in her life she wept in this man's arms, wept for a love that was lost, for the empty ache of that loss. And he held her closely, cradling her head into the protective span of his shoulder, and she clung to the strange, bittersweet comfort, the past with its legacy of shame and humiliation obliterated in this hiatus of human warmth and understanding.

At last Venetia's sobs subsided, leaving her feeling drained yet oddly at peace, and into the emptiness something else crept, like a thief, wickedly stealing away all those carefully impressed mental defences. She had told herself that he meant nothing to her now, that the love she had believed to be deathless had been nothing but a fantasy conjured from the wild imaginings of a silly teenager. She had told herself so often, so determinedly, that she had had no option but to believe it.

But now her body was telling her something else entirely, told her that she was instinctively tuned to the pace of his heartbeat, the rhythm of his breathing, the scent, the warmth, the uniqueness of him. And responding to it all, like a tight bud unfurling in the warmth of the sun, shedding the defensive carapace she had so carefully constructed to cover the emotional wound of loving him so long ago. And exposed the pain of the lacerations that hadn't been forgotten at all, and it was raw, sharp, craving the fulfilment he had denied before, blatantly begging with every hot pulse-beat, each invitingly peaked nipple, each enervating wave of melting, languorous, naked desire.

And she went very still in his arms, incapable of fighting the wonder of this, able only to understand it because, surely, it was inevitable. And she felt him hold his breath, and then the sharp exhalation of air, his voice controlled, edged with just the faintest hint of derision as he removed her clinging hands from around his neck and set her gently back against the pillows, his mouth curling as he said, 'What a strange enigma you are, Venetia. I came to your room, expecting what I found—a seductive woman who had been thwarted in her intention to spend the night in her lover's arms.' The mocking, denigrating gleam had reappeared in his hooded eyes as he stood up, shrugging the fabric of his dark, beautifully made Italian suit more comfortably around his impressive shoulders. 'Wearing a slinky slither of erotic satin, reading a sexy novel to compensate for all that frustration. Only to have you sobbing like a child in my arms, revealing your soul.' Again, the minimal shrug, the lean, wicked grace of the man as he slid his hands into the pockets of his trousers, his tailored jacket parting to show the unmistakable patches where her uncontrolled tears had watered his shirt. 'I had not thought you had a soul.'

The frightening change in him made her shudder, pull the duvet up to her chin, her slanting eyes a luminous pearly blue, misted with incomprehension. Until she got her mind back into some sort of order, understanding too well, and shot sharply at him, 'Simon is not my——'

'Don't lie,' he interrupted harshly, the line of his mouth a castigation in itself. 'If you and Carew weren't lovers six years ago, you were on the brink. That much, from where I stood, was inevitable. And despite the fact that he has a wife, the closeness between the two of you today was unmissable.'

There was not a lot she could say in her own defence. Nothing short enough, telling enough to cut through those deep-rooted misconceptions with the immediacy of truth. And why should she bother, anyway? she asked drearily inside her head. What did any of it matter?

But it still stung unbearably when he turned his back on her and strode to the door as if he couldn't bear to breathe the same air one moment longer, and the sting of it, the hopelessness of it, coalesced into a moment of sheer, miserable mortification when he paused in the doorway and taunted, 'I'll ask Potty to bring you fresh hot soup, and a tot of brandy to help you sleep. If I come near you again tonight we might both forget I'm not a married man.'

The cruelty of that parting shot had been understandable, Venetia rationalised as she dressed the following morning. Hadn't she told him herself that she 'only played with married men'? The impulsive stupidity of that slice of bravado made her cringe with self-contempt.

Pulling on a warm cream-coloured sweater to top the neat grey skirt she had dragged haphazardly from the wardrobe, she applied a discreet amount of make-up and told herself to set the record straight, make him believe in her sexual integrity, at least.

She was not eighteen any more, and what she had done six years ago—although unbelievably embarrassing in retrospect—had at least been honest. She had truly believed herself to be in love with him.

Whereas yesterday she had deliberately acted out a lie. Her behaviour had been cheap, not to mention totally unfair to Simon who, as far as she knew, had not the least desire to cheat on his wife and would be justifiably enraged and disgusted if he ever discovered just how she had implicated him!

She could only put that dreadful aberration—not to mention the later moment of madness when, in his arms, she had mistakenly believed that her idiotic teenage infatuation was still alive and kicking—down to her mental exhaustion, her continuing state of shock over the death of her beloved father. One evening he'd been with her, idly discussing her working day, suggesting a game of chess since there'd been nothing on television either of them wanted to watch, his usual calm, loving self. The next morning he'd been gone. He'd slipped away in the night with no one to hold his hand, to comfort him, no one to say goodbye.

Pushing such weakening memories aside, she made her bed and tidied her room while she got herself back under control. Tomorrow she would go into the office, get back to normal, and today she would tell Carlo the truth. She had to do that, if only to regain her self-respect. But,

'He left over an hour ago,' Potty said in answer to Venetia's enquiries. 'So what would you like for breakfast? And don't tell me you're not hungry again. I'll give in my notice if you do, and that's a fact!'

Although she knew the threat was hollow, Venetia gave in. She was going to have to force herself to eat. She would be ill if she didn't, and that wouldn't help anyone. So she said unenthusiastically, 'Anything. Toast, fruit, cereal—whatever's going, I don't mind.' She paced the big, comfortable kitchen edgily, wishing she could pin the cause of these bouts of restlessness down, and asked, she hoped offhandedly, 'Has he gone for good? Carlo, I mean. Did he take his luggage with him?' And she wondered why she felt calmer, why the upsurge of relief was so strangely sweet when the housekeeper scoffed,

'No, of course not. He said he'd be back some time this afternoon. I think he'll be around for some days—probably weeks. He's keeping an eye on you, looking after you like the nice man he is.'

But even through the incomprehensible glow of relief there was a sharp edge to Venetia's voice as she countered, 'Keeping an eye on the business, more like. Looking after his shareholding.'

And earned herself a withering look and a terse, 'Eat your breakfast.'

Suppressing a sigh of irritation, Venetia resigned herself to tackling the lot—hot oatmeal, a thick slice of toasted granary bread, and the fruit bowl. And, with Potty's eagle eye watching every mouthful, she managed to eat more at one sitting than she had done for the past week. And when she emphatically refused a second piece of fruit Potty whisked the used china from the table, untied her apron, and said, 'You won't mind if I buzz off now, will you? I haven't visited Enid in a fortnight and she'll begin to get narky. I'll catch the ten o'clock bus and be back by four, in good time to get dinner.'

'I'll run you over in the car.' Venetia pushed her chair back from the table. Potty's older widowed sister lived a mere handful of miles away, on the outskirts of the neighbouring market town. She suffered from arthritis and didn't get about much and if Potty missed one of her regular visits Enid got maudlin, accusing her sister of not caring what happened to her, sending Potty to the far end of her tether. 'And no need to rush back,' she added. 'I can start dinner. I'm giving the office a miss for today. Just phone me when you want me to collect you.'

If she sold this house, as Simon had already advised, and moved into a flat in the suburbs of London, she would have to take Potty with her. It wouldn't be nearly so easy for her to visit her sister, and there would be ructions, which might be a problem.

But there was no way she could abandon the woman who had been like a second mother to her for twenty-four years. Finding another job at her age wouldn't be easy, and she knew she wouldn't be able to stand living with her sister, seeing her every day, all day.

The immediate future was still on her mind when she garaged the car and walked back into the house a little over half an hour later. Selling up would be a terrible wrench but, as Simon had pointed out, the wine retail business was having a hard time and extra working capital was vital. In order to even begin thinking of competing with the big supermarket chains, they needed to buy in huge, discounted quantities. Only that way could they compete on a price level, keep branches open and staff in work. And the capital had to come from somewhere; they were already over their borrowing limit with the bank and unless she and Simon could come up with a miracle the house and its contents would have to go.

Her brow furrowed, she left her coat and boots in the cubby-hole off the main hall and rubbed her hands together. It was bitterly cold outside, the wind raw and cutting, and even with the central heating in here she was still shivering as she went to the study to phone Simon.

She had half promised herself to contact him today, and if he was free for lunch she could drive into town and they could discuss the whole problem rationally, try to find a solution that wouldn't entail actually having to sell up, uproot herself and Potty.

Phoning through to Simon's office, Venetia glanced at her watch. If Simon was free she would have just about enough time to change and drive into town. Then she felt her face go hot as Carlo's unmistakable tones clipped down the wire.

'I want to speak to Simon.' The words were pushed out without much thought.

The unexpectedness of hearing him speak had scrambled her brain and she knew she must have sounded like a petulant child, and his terse 'Why?' didn't help, made her bite out crossly,

'I don't think that's any of your business, do you?'

'No?' His tone was infuriatingly patronising and Venetia had to fight the impulse to crash the receiver back on its rest, and clenched her teeth as he continued, his voice silky-smooth, 'If you give me your message, I'll see he gets it. That's if it's fit for third-party consumption.' Which had her snapping back, enraged by his uncalled for allusion, because why the heck should he care if she was having affairs with half the men in London?

'I would like to meet him for lunch. Just tell him the usual place, one o'clock,' she said, and left him to make what he liked of that. She wasn't going to demean herself, beg him to believe she and Simon needed to have a private business discussion.

And she could swear she heard a purr in that deep, sexy voice when he came back, 'Ah—lunch. Unfortunately, he and I are deep in last year's accounts and are likely to remain so until well into the afternoon. I'll see you later.'

The line went dead and she knew, she just knew, that he had taken a devilish delight in putting her down. She really would like to throttle him with one of his own immaculate silk ties!

And what right had he to be going through the books without her express say-so? Or to dictate how Simon, the firm's highest paid and most respected employee, should spend his lunch hour? And why should he have taken so much pleasure in preventing her and Simon from spending time together?

She knew that Carlo must have a string of affairs behind him, stretching way back into the past, so who was he to take such a high moral tone over her supposed ongoing affair with her PA? Anyone would think he had a personal interest—which was just plain ridiculous!

Ten minutes later she was calm enough to recall that Simon had warned her that Carlo had demanded a meeting with him today, and a general management meeting tomorrow. If she had remembered she wouldn't have even thought of suggesting she and Simon meet for lunch.

And he did have rights, of course he did. He owned practically half the company and was, sensibly, looking after his interests, not calling her in on any discussions until the following day when, with the trauma of the funeral forty-eight hours behind her, she could be expected to bring her full concentration to the business in hand.

And she had blown it again, unthinkingly adding to his misconceptions about her relationship with Simon. She was going to have to tell him the truth this evening, even if it meant going back six years to that dreadful day when he had found them, to all intents and purposes, in the middle of a torrid love scene by the pool.

Thwarted in her intention to reach a decision on whether she should sell her home or not, the rest of the day stretched emptily ahead. And, although she had no taste for it, she used the time to go through her father's papers. It was a painful exercise but it had to be done, and when the phone extension in the study rang out she was grateful for the interruption.

Pushing the pile of papers to be kept into a drawer of the desk, she lifted the receiver, glancing at her watch. Three o'clock, and the time had passed unbelievably quickly, and when she heard Potty say, 'It's me. Is that you?' she smiled and answered.

'No, it's the tooth fairy. Do you want me to collect you already? I told you not to rush. But if Enid's been giving you a hard time I'll come straight over.'

'Where have you been all day?' Potty wanted to know. 'Sitting in a corner with a bag over your head? Look out of the window.'

Frowning, Venetia swivelled the chair round to face the French windows behind her, her eyes widening as she registered the white-out, and Potty told her, 'It's been throwing it down for the last three hours. I'd have come back on the bus but it doesn't run until half-three, and the state the roads are in it won't run at all. And I don't want you risking it, so if it's all right with you I'll stay put for tonight. Is Signor Rossi back?'

'No, he's not. And of course you must stay where you are. I've been going through Dad's papers; I had no idea it was snowing——'

'Which proves you didn't bother to get yourself any lunch,' the housekeeper grumbled. 'I don't like the idea of you being on your own. But perhaps——' her dour tone lightened '—the *signor*'s already on his way back and——'

'I doubt it,' Venetia interrupted in her turn. 'He'd have more sense. And don't worry, I'm perfectly capable of looking after myself. See you when the roads are passable.'

Standing, stretching to ease the stiffness from her limbs, Venetia wondered why she should so suddenly feel the weight of disappointment press so firmly down upon her, and why, going over to the windows to look out on the countryside which was heavily blanketed with the snow that had been threatened for days, she should feel it had fallen simply to spite her!

She should, she told herself with a spurt of exasperation, be crowing with blessed relief, because Carlo would undoubtedly get a room in town and leave her in peace!

She would enjoy her enforced isolation, she adjured herself firmly. If it killed her! She wouldn't mope, she wouldn't grieve, and she certainly wouldn't miss Carlo's exasperating presence!

So she lit a fire in the small sitting-room, made herself a pot of tea which she drank in the kitchen, and assembled the ingredients for a lasagne, then opened a bottle of red wine.

She enjoyed cooking, somewhat to her own surprise, and had discovered its therapeutic qualities when one evening, shortly after she'd first joined the family business, she'd returned home feeling wound up to the point of explosion. And Potty had taken one look at her and advised, 'Try your hand at a chocolate cake. I'll give you my secret recipe. You'd be surprised how beating and whisking and admiring the results can calm a body down.'

And she was enjoying herself now, she told herself as she briskly grated cheese for the sauce. She was quite content to be pottering around on her own for once and quietly grateful for the fact that she would not have to endure Carlo's despotic company, his savagely cutting remarks.

So quite why her heart should perform a double somersault and then go on to patter as if she'd just run to the top of Everest and back when he walked into the kitchen, she just didn't know, and sensibly put it down to the unexpectedness of seeing him here, his black hair clinging damply to his skull, his Italian-styled black wool overcoat spangled with snowflakes.

The way he was looking at her made her feel threatened, as if she was trapped, had no place of safety to run to. He was big and dark and dangerous, and the black glitter of his eyes, the slight, predatory curl of his sensual mouth, contained a message she had no wish to translate, and so she said quickly, her voice thick with accusation, her tongue running away from her, divorced from her brain, 'Why did you come back?' And the lump of cheese she'd been so industriously grating dropped from her fingers, her face running with hot colour as she received an answer she didn't like the sound of at all.

'To take care of some unfinished business, of course. Did you really think I wouldn't come back to claim what you were so generously offering six years ago?'

CHAPTER FIVE

'I DON'T know what you're talking about,' Venetia lied frantically, busying herself with the sauce. That had been a rotten thing to say, and she kept her back to him because she knew her face was like a burning beacon. 'I was merely making conversation—though I can't think why I bothered. I'd have thought you would have had enough sense to stay in town tonight, considering the state of the roads.'

'Ah.' He sounded amused. 'I think you know only too well what I was talking about. However, if we must change the conversation, we must.' He was coming closer; she could feel it in every last inch of her body. Her hands began to shake and she bit her lip, making herself concentrate on the task in hand as his voice washed over her, soft as silk, 'Did you imagine a mere snowstorm would keep me away? I don't think you know me at all.'

So why did that sound sinister? No reason. She was letting her imagination run away with her. Sensing his presence at her shoulder, she stirred the contents of the pan furiously, holding her breath, because even the slightest variation in the rhythm of her breathing could give her away, show him how achingly aware of him he could make her.

'You have changed, Venetia.' Idly he lifted a hand and hooked the forward-falling wing of dark hair back behind her ear, and she wanted to snap, Don't touch me! but that, too, would have given her away.

'When I first met you, you were thoroughly undomesticated; you wouldn't have known a duster from an egg-whisk. All I ever saw you do was paint your nails and lounge around the pool—with the occasional dash upstairs to change into something even more flamboyant. What brought about such a radical alteration, I wonder?'

If she told him he wouldn't believe it, she thought tartly, taking the pan off the burner. Loving him had changed her; discovering that she couldn't automatically have exactly what she wanted, when she wanted it, had changed her.

'Nothing to say?' His eyes mocked her. 'Then I shall have the pleasure of finding out, won't I? One way or another.' He gave a small, curling smile that made her spine tingle, and then he turned and strode arrogantly from the room, and Venetia let out a long sigh of ragged breath and pressed her fingers to her temples.

This man spelled danger. The combination of threat and sensuality was shattering. No wonder loving him had changed her, the change going much deeper than surface level. On the surface there was the sleeker, trimmer self, the lushness fined down to a willowy grace, the hedonistic girl becoming a calm, dedicated career woman.

But underneath there was more; the change went deeper. In the still, stark days after she'd watched him walk away she had come to a new understanding of how her life was going to have to be. The ebullience of youth had passed with his going, the sheer, unthinking confidence mown down by the threshing knives of his rejection, and she had known then that life was not one long, glorious party.

That was when the stronger, more reflective Venetia had emerged. Never again was she going to throw her love away on any man. The family business, the family home would be her life, and if she ever married it would be for all the right reasons; for companionship, mutual respect and affection. Children, maybe; she hadn't yet got round to thinking that far ahead.

Opening up the gate-legged table in the smaller of the two sitting-rooms where she had chosen to light a fire to boost the central heating on this bitterly cold night, she wondered how she was going to get through this evening without Potty to act as a buffer between her and Carlo. He frightened her.

Or rather, she admitted with severe honesty, her physical reaction to him frightened her.

Whenever he came near her her pulse-rate soared, and that had to be the bitter legacy of the juvenile infatuation she had believed to be dead and buried. Whenever he was in her vicinity she had the enervating impression of *déjà vu*, and she was going to have to get to grips with it somehow.

'Can I help?' His voice from the doorway had her swivelling round, and she made herself meet those wicked black eyes with cool formality. He had changed into a soft midnight-blue cashmere sweater and close-fitting black trousers, and he looked every inch a predator, and despite all her good intentions her wayward mind recalled how it felt to be held by those strong arms, the velvet threat in his voice when he'd told her he'd come back to claim what she had offered six years ago.

And that was enough to have her blushing to the roots of her hair, more than enough. He smiled laconically, as if he could read her mind, and she looked away quickly, snapping out more forcefully than his offer merited, 'No, thanks. Everything's ready. I only have to carry it through.' And she swept out of the room before he could offer to do it for her, his low laughter following, making her grind her teeth.

It was going to be a difficult evening, no doubt about it. He was in a Machiavellian mood and was obviously going to enjoy rubbing her nose in the dirt of her wanton behaviour all those years ago. He was no gentleman!

But despite her fearful misgivings, dinner was an easy meal. The wine helped, of course, but mostly it was down to his uncontentious, relaxing conversation, she decided, wondering if she had misjudged him. And then, unwittingly, she led in the wrong direction when, after telling him how Potty had got herself stranded with the whinging Enid, she confided, 'When she moves to London with me—and I don't think she'll have much option, not to begin with—it will take her hours to get back to the village to visit her sister using public transport. I can't see her tackling the journey too often. There will be a few tantrums from our Enid.'

'And why should you move to London?' His intent stare was grim, unyielding, and Venetia cursed her unguarded tongue. Discussing her future plans with him was the last thing she had meant to do. The business was hers, and her moves to ensure its future were private, between Simon—in his capacity as her adviser—and herself. But to brush it off, to lie, to pretend she wanted to move to where the bright lights were, would only further lower his rock-bottom opinion of her. And she had already done enough damage in that direction.

So, reluctantly, she told him, 'As you have to be aware, the business is crying out for an injection of capital if we're going to keep branches open and people in work. The sale of this house and its contents would answer that need.'

'And have I no say in this madness?' He lifted his eyebrows but, despite the almost dispassionate tone of his voice, his accent, she noted, was a little more pronounced than usual. She shook her head.

'Not really. No.' She wasn't looking at him now, because something in the intentness of his level gaze was making her heart beat frantically, either with fear or excitement, she didn't know which, because she couldn't be objective enough to judge.

The filter coffee-maker was chuntering to itself on the low, polished oak Elizabethan sideboard, and she got up swiftly from the table, filling two cups, and when she turned again he said decisively, 'I cannot allow you to do anything so rash. What will happen when that money's gone? Not only will you be in exactly the same position as you are now, but you will have no valuable assets to dispose of. Nothing.'

'Simon and I have plans,' she informed him loftily, slapping his cup down in front of him. 'Why be so defeatist?'

'Simon and I,' he mocked with slow deliberation, twisting his wine glass idly round with the tips of his long fingers. 'I imagine he has ideas aplenty. Especially if they prolong his highly paid employment and finance his buying trips abroad. I repeat, I cannot allow you to act so rashly.'

Venetia felt her tenuous hold on her self-control begin to fall apart, and before she could do anything stupid, like scream at him and tell him to go boil his inflated head, she downed the remainder of the wine in her glass, swallowing her ire along with the dregs, and was able to clip out, more or less steadily, 'I'm afraid you have no right to dictate to me in this matter. After probate's been granted, this house and its contents will be mine, to do with as I please.' And there was nothing he could do about that, was there?

Without knowing it, her slanting eyes were mockingly triumphant, challenging him to argue with that, and she was totally unprepared for his silky, 'If it weren't for the fact that I promised your father I'd look out for you and your interests I would happily watch you walk to hell in your own way.' He stretched back in his chair, both hands clasped behind his head, his eyes half-closed as he watched the way her colour came and went, leaving her paler than before. 'However, as that promise was made, and as my own business interests are also concerned, I am prepared to offer two options.'

'How kind!' Sarcasm sharpened her voice. She knew her father had maintained close contact with Carlo after his visit. Since the ending of the old family feud he had seemed doubly anxious to keep in touch, to make up for the long years when the family had split, their branch anglicising the Italian Rossi to Ross.

But what on earth had possessed her father to ask this devil to watch out for her? Hadn't he trusted her ability to look after herself, to carry on the business as he had done?

'I agree.' Carlo's hooded eyes followed her every movement as she rose jerkily to her feet, stacking their plates. 'My magnanimity sometimes amazes me.'

His almost insolent drawl was too much to bear, she thought, compressing her mouth as she turned to walk out on him, taking the dishes. But, without even seeing him make a move, she felt the steel band of his fingers around her wrist, and the china fell back to the table with an ominous clatter. And she met the malevolent glitter of his eyes across the debris of what had been a surprisingly pleasant meal and knew that the last flimsy veils of polite pretence had been ripped away forever.

Knew it and faced it as he rose elegantly to his feet, his hand still shackling her in that merciless grip as he led her with all the superiority of his ingrained male arrogance to the plump two-seater sofa which flanked one side of the brightly burning fire.

To attempt to escape, to fight her way out of this room, would be both undignified and futile, Venetia realised. Unwittingly she had brought this hornet's nest down on her head, and now she had to suffer the consequences.

And now wasn't the time to put him straight about her supposed relationship with Simon, was it? He would see her attempts to exonerate herself—to explain that when she'd said she only played with married men it had been a piece of arrant bravado, a defence mechanism to hide her embarrassment at the shameful memories his unexpected presence had evoked—as an irritating irrelevance.

At the moment he was only interested in the business, and somehow she had to make him believe that she was capable of making her own decisions, good ones, that his promise to look after her could be put into cold storage.

But he was much too close for her to be able to think clearly; his nearness always had this disastrous effect on her equilibrium and she inched carefully away on the soft cushions, fighting a furious battle for inner control, sensing his eyes on her stony profile.

Keep calm, she instructed herself tightly, otherwise he'll trample all over you, try to take the control of the business out of your hands. Then she told him, her tone as reasonable as she could make it, 'I see no point at all in this continual arguing. Maybe if I put my plans for the business on the table we might be able to discuss them like rational human beings.'

'What an agreeable idea.' His voice was silky smooth yet his fingers, as they grasped her chin, were hard as steel. He turned her head. 'Look at me when you speak to me, Venetia.'

His eyes held hers with a force that left her breathless, almost incapable of movement, and when he said softly, teasingly, 'Go on, you have my complete attention,' she had to haul herself away from the bewildering sensation of drowning.

Pushing her muddled thoughts into some sort of order, she said quickly, 'In the past we've bought widely, using a diversity of shippers and vine owners. But I plan . . .' She broke off awkwardly, bemused by the expression on his face. His heavy lids were half lowered over those magnificent black eyes and a small smile played along the long, sensual line of his mouth, played with her foolish senses.

Venetia took in a short, sharp breath, the tip of her tongue moistening her parched lips as she closed her eyes just briefly, marshalling her wits. He must think her a fool, not capable of running a dolls' tea-party, let alone a business that had retail outlets in most major towns in the UK.

'I intend,' she continued more firmly, evading his eyes again, 'to buy almost exclusively from Rossi. The larger orders would qualify for discounts we could pass on to our customers and so compete with the big supermarket chains. It would also be to Rossi's advantage, so both ways you would win. You would sell more wine to us, and through us, and you, as a part-owner of Ross UK, would benefit because of our increased profitability.'

'Does Carew agree to your proposals?' he asked, raising his eyebrows, and at his gently sardonic tone her slanting eyes slid back to his.

Why bring Simon into the discussion at this stage? If a deal was struck it would be between Ross UK and Rossi International and then, with her proposal agreed to in principle, the interested parties would have their accountants and solicitors thrash out the details. Simon would be instructed to alter his buying patterns when everything had been sorted out.

'I haven't discussed it with him,' she replied stiffly, wishing she had. But the idea had only struck her after his suggestion that she liquidise her considerable assets, after probate, and inject the much needed capital into the business. She respected Simon's judgement, as her father had, and would have thrashed out the pros and cons of her brainwave with him before putting it formally to Rossi International. She would have talked it over with him at lunch today, had she been able to, and now she had been pitchforked into telling Carlo what was on her mind.

But surely he could only agree?

'So Carew is still in the dark? I see,' he said mildly, as if she had somehow answered an unspoken question. 'However, what if I don't agree?'

'Why shouldn't you?' Her narrowed eyes swept the handsome austerity of his face, but his features might have been hewn from stone for all the enlightenment they gave her. 'Granted, I haven't worked out the details, but surely, in principle——'

'In principle I disagree most strongly with the way you intend raising the necessary capital,' he interrupted inflexibly. 'I've already explained why.' He leaned back into the angle of the sofa, his eyes very dark in the olive tones of his skin as he regarded her with level assessment. And Venetia tightened her mouth; it seemed he was determined to block her every move, and she didn't know why.

'As part-owner of the business, and sole owner of Rossi, I would have thought you would have jumped at the idea. After all,' she reminded tartly, 'I'm not asking you to raise the capital!'

'Quite so,' he remarked idly, his eyes lazy, like a drowsing predator, his casual attitude to her problem making her anger impossible to control as she bit right back,

'Then maybe I should find some other major wine shipper to work out a deal with, since it's obvious you'd rather sit back and watch branches close down, see people thrown out of their jobs!' He was impossible to deal with, and if his ancestors had been anything like him then she could fully understand why hers had split!

'You misjudge me.' His smile was slow and easy, but she had more sense than to take that, or his words, at face value.

'Is that so?' She raised one perfectly arched eyebrow disdainfully and saw his smile broaden into a grin that could stop the entire female population of the planet in their tracks.

'Obviously. My share in your business is a very tiny part of my empire. But, as you should know by now, I relinquish nothing.' And no one, not even you, his eyes seemed to add, and Venetia shook her head briskly to rid herself of that product of an over-fevered imagination. 'However, if you recall, I told you I had two options to put to you. Interested?'

'Naturally.' What else could she say? she thought, making the replenishment of the fire her excuse for putting distance between them. He might even have thought of a way out that she hadn't seen, she decided, tossing more logs on to the embers. She could at least listen to what he had to say; she didn't necessarily have to agree with it.

'We marry, and bring Ross UK under the wide and accommodating umbrella of my company.'

Venetia straightened slowly, dusting her hands off, her back still to him as she willed the heated rush of colour to fade. Six years ago she would have given all she possessed to hear him propose marriage. And, even now, emotions she had thought to be buried deep in her memory flared to vibrant life, shocking her with the intensity of their unwanted rebirth, and it was some seconds before she felt composed enough to ask coolly, 'And the second option? It has to be better than the first.' How could he have so cold-bloodedly proposed marriage, for business reasons only? He didn't like her and he certainly didn't respect her! Did he really think she would be willing to agree to such an empty union? Or was he playing games?

'Better? It depends on your viewpoint,' he murmured as she reluctantly turned to face him, doing her best to hide her hectic reactions to his outrageous proposal. 'If the idea of becoming my wife is so repugnant to you, then the second option comes into effect. My company will cease to do business with you, and you will find yourself boycotted by most, if not all, of the major wine exporters.'

'You can't do that!' Venetia whispered, hardly able to believe she was hearing this.

But he nodded slowly. 'Would you like to put me to the test?'

The assurance in his deep voice sent shivers scudding down her spine and she heard him say, as if through a blanket of icy mist, 'You could continue to trade, of course, but at a price. Very soon the money you could raise would be gone, the least profitable of your outlets would have to be sold to shore up the remainder, and on and on until you were left with so little that I would be able to step in and buy up the tatty remains, and you would be begging me to take them off your hands. In short, my dear, I would starve you out.'

Although she was shaking inside she faced him, her spine as rigid as she could make it. There was a still, hard confidence about him, something cold and intent looking out of his eyes. He meant every word he had said, and he would break her with as little compunction as he would step on an insect. Break her or marry her. And there was only one question to be asked, and she asked it, letting the thick veil of dark lashes descend to hide the shock in her eyes. 'Why?'

His immediate response was silence, a silence so intense that she was shaken by it, the tension inside her building to breaking-point. She knew she must be visibly trembling, and when he told her softly, 'That, my dear, is for me to know, and you to discover,' she shot him a distraught, frenzied glance and started for the door.

She had to get away from him, from this crazy nightmare. She had to think things through. But he levered himself off the sofa with deceptive indolence and blocked her blindly chosen escape route with his hard body.

For a moment she couldn't think straight, her breath frozen in her lungs, but when she felt the heat of his hands on her shoulders she began to fight, lashing out at him with her feet and fists in anguished desperation, one tiny, objective part of her brain asking her why she didn't simply and coolly demand time to consider his proposal of marriage, or threaten to lodge an official complaint of blackmail against him.

But his demeaning offer of marriage had woken emotions that had become wildly distorted during the long years of their burial, and fighting him was the only way she could begin to cope with them, because he had brought them to clamouring, insistent life. He was responsible. He had to be punished.

Frenziedly, she lifted her fists to beat him out of the way, and she knew, in that moment of madness, that she would kill him if she could, kill him for being the man he was, the man she had loved, the man who had hurt her beyond bearing and would hurt her again without a second thought. And, dimly, she heard him swear, then felt his arms go round her, pinning her with subduing force to the hard, vital length of his body.

'*Basta*!' The expletive hissed through his teeth. 'Be still. You are going to hurt yourself.'

'Let me go! I hate you!' she spat at him, her eyes wild as she tried to wriggle free, using her fists, knees, elbows, her body as tight as a bow. But as one hand hauled her more tightly against him the other tangled in her hair, pulling her head back, and she was forced to meet the volcanic passion of his eyes as he grated with vehement force,

'Once you said you loved me.' His lips drew back against his teeth. 'Love, hate, it's all the same.' And he kissed her with a hard brutality that shocked her into stillness.

Venetia trembled, knowing it was useless to try to challenge his formidable strength, as the ravishing pressure of his mouth dominated her senses. She could feel the hard, heated muscles of his perfect body pressing against her own, and the sensation was weakening, sapping her strength. With an anguished moan, she twisted her head, but his grip merely tightened, his mouth marauding, devouring hers.

He was demanding a response and she wasn't giving it, and she uncurled her fists, trying to push him away, but the feel of the firm, strongly arching ribcage beneath her palms had her catching her breath in a sob as a dark tide of febrile desire coursed violently through her veins.

She was back in time, back where she had always been, had she but known it, back to the moment of knowing she had met the man she would love all her life. The moment of immediate need, desire and adoration, the endless moment that meant she had come full circle. And she was responding now, responding as she had dreamed of doing all those years ago, with all the fiery passion of her nature, the fire and the passion raging out of control after that long, cold, lonely immurement.

And she was fighting again, but this time it was different. She was fighting for the freedom to love, the freedom to adore him with her hands, her lips, her body. And after a second when his body grew still, tension holding him rigid as she slipped her eager, searching hands beneath the soft wool of his sweater, he matched her pagan, sensual needs, matched and outstripped them until she was panting in his arms, somehow back on the sofa, somehow without a stitch of clothing between them.

The firelight flickered and gleamed on the oiled silk of his body; he was, quite simply, magnificent. Venetia groaned and reached for him, but he put his mouth on hers and murmured thickly, 'Softly, *cara*. Softly.' And kissed her gently, with tantalising slowness, tasting her, sucking lazily on the inviting lushness of her mouth, quietening her with drugging sensation.

And slowly, in the soft golden firelight, the tormenting ecstasy continued as his mouth discovered every inch of her body, his hands gentling her as she twisted and writhed, glorying in her need for him. She cradled his head in her hands, her fingertips biting through the thick dark softness of his hair, and heard him utter hoarsely, 'I've dreamed of this so many times. Of possessing you, taking you, taming you...' With a savage groan he buried his head between her breasts, and Venetia went very still as she repeated, articulating with difficulty,

'Taming me, is that all?' Nothing about loving, about the needs of the heart, the yearning? Furious with herself, more than with him, she tried to push him away.

And he answered her thickly, 'Not all. Not by any means.' He levered himself up on his elbow, shifting his body slightly, half covering hers now, his black eyes clouded as he told her, 'You were eighteen years old when you made me ache to possess you. Think of it—for the first time in my life I burned for the unattainable; is it any wonder I felt I could no longer control my destiny? Is it any wonder I fought that alarming and totally new experience?'

She saw the rueful half-smile in the fireglow and opened her mouth to protest that she hadn't been unattainable at all, far from it, but he laid a finger over her lips, sealing them, telling her, his accent more pronounced now than she had ever heard it, 'There I was, a mature adult male, pole-axed by a girl scarcely out of the schoolroom and, what was worse, a girl who, in her newly emerging sexuality, imagined herself in love with me! Who was openly willing to allow me to lead her over the threshold into the realms of true womanhood. *Cristo*! How I was tempted! How my days and nights were torn apart with dreaming of how it could be—of how I wanted it to be!' His mouth turned down wryly as he dipped his head. 'I'm sorry. I had not intended to rush you, to leap on you like an animal.' And then, with a coldness that took her breath away, 'Is the idea of being my wife so truly repugnant to you?'

'No,' she answered quickly, frowning a little. Then took the option he had tacitly offered and began to wriggle back into her clothing, being extra careful not to look at him, because, naked, he was superb, far too tempting.

Venetia knew she had to be careful. A few moments ago she would have welcomed him as her lover without a thought in her head. Reason and logic slid out of the back door under such sensual onslaughts. She wished she knew what he was thinking. But even six years ago he had been adept at hiding his feelings—if what he had just told her was the truth. At the time he had behaved as if she were an irritating, unamusing child.

The silence was dense, broken only by the rustle of her clothing and, she was sure, the pattering of her frantic heartbeats. And into the silence he said abruptly, 'Am I to take that as an acceptance of my proposal?'

Startled, she stood up, her eyes reflecting her confusion as they met the intent blackness of his, and she had to bite her tongue to contain the breathless, unthinking affirmative. Like the man himself, his offer was much too tempting. She knew he found her physically attractive—he couldn't have faked his reaction of just a few minutes ago—but, loving him, could she settle for that?

'It's too big a step to take lightly,' she told him with forced clarity, and stepped into her shoes. 'Give me time to think about it.'

'Time to decide whether the success of your father's company and job security for all those employees is worth the sacrifice of having to remain faithful to just one man for the rest of your life?' he shot at her cynically, getting to his feet, magnificently male, totally unashamed of his nakedness, or unaware of it. And Venetia closed her eyes, fighting back the insane urge to weep because that was how he saw her and his offer to marry her had been made for two reasons only. Firstly to bring back the errant and ailing company under the paternal Rossi umbrella, and secondly to honour that promise he'd made to her father.

'And be very sure, Venetia,' his voice came darkly, 'that, as your husband, I would demand total fidelity, until the very last breath in your body.' He began, unhurriedly, to dress, and the unvoiced threat darkened the room. Venetia shuddered. He was so utterly sure of himself, of his ability to dominate her, and there was too much to say, to ask, too many misguided impressions to correct.

She didn't know how to begin and wasn't sure if it was worth the effort, because he would never afford her the respect she needed, give her the love she craved so desperately. He had suggested marriage because it suited his business plans and allowed him to honour his promise to her father. The fact that the physical chemistry between them was undeniable would, as far as he was concerned, be a bonus.

Unconsciously she shook her head, silently refusing everything—both the heaven and the hell—and Carlo, gathering his shoes and soft cashmere sweater, told her tightly, 'You have until tomorrow to reach a decision. If there is to be a wedding I want to announce it at the management meeting in the morning. It would calm the rumours of insolvency and reassure all concerned.' And he went to bed. Alone.

CHAPTER SIX

ALONE. Venetia had never felt so alone in her life, not even when she'd been trying to come to terms with the shock of her father's death.

She stared round the spotless kitchen, her shoulders slumped. She had cleared away the debris of their meal, washed down all the surfaces, and there was nothing left to do here unless she opted to go down on hands and knees and scrub the already immaculate floor.

It was past one in the morning, but she couldn't bear the thought of going to bed, lying awake and staring into the darkness, knowing that Carlo was not far away, sleeping, his conscience not troubling him one iota, his future unclouded by fear, because he could handle being tied to a woman he didn't love and couldn't respect. Their marriage would reunite the family again, suit his business plans and, without a single qualm, he would make love to her whenever he felt the urge—just until he tired of her, until the novelty of 'possessing and taming' her had worn off.

Never mind the pain and heartbreak such a marriage would inflict on her, the tawdry sensation of being used—both physically and for practical business purposes. He could handle it, no problem. His emotions would be untouched while hers would be ripped to shreds because she loved the brute.

Yet what alternative did she have?

Venetia compressed her mouth and made her way upstairs through the silent house. She could always tell him to get lost, stick to her original plans for trying to secure the business and fight him when he carried out his threat to starve her out.

She knew she was strong enough to fight him on that level, using all her grit and determination to hang on grimly to the bitter end, conceding—when she had to—only slowly, digging her heels in, making him sweat for his victory.

But did she have the right to put all those jobs at risk? And was she strong enough to fight her most fearsome enemy—herself?

Her brain might tell her that marriage to Carlo would bring nothing but the heartbreak of unreturned love, the agony and frustration of watching him growing ever more distant once the fires of his physical lust had been doused by the cold waters of familiarity and indifference. But her heart, her flesh, seemed strangers to reason, aching for him, logic consumed in the incandescent flames of blind love and sheer, terrifying need. Could she be strong enough to fight that?

Grimly she paced her bedroom floor, too restless and edgy to think of trying to sleep. Carlo would demand his answer in the morning and unless she got her head together she wouldn't be able to give him one. She was being torn apart, her mind urging her to take the cautious path of self-protection, her heart and body aching for the exquisite ecstasy of belonging wholly to him, no matter how fleetingly and damagingly.

Uncharacteristically, she swore aloud, surprising—almost shocking—herself by her own harsh utterance of the blistering word. Then she grabbed a thickly padded coat from the wardrobe, a pair of warm cords, and changed quickly, pulling on calf-height leather boots. Maybe an hour's brisk exercise in the cold, bright night air would clear her head, enable her to judge the situation sensibly. At the very least, it would work off some of this surplus nervous energy, allow her to sleep for a few hours.

There had been a light frost and the snow was crisp underfoot, the full moon riding high overhead, gliding through gauzy clouds, touching the gardens with enchantment. Venetia filled her lungs with the pure cold air, stuffed her hands in the pockets of her anorak, and set off, down across the lawns to the water garden, cutting through to the perimeter wall by way of the nut-walk, then out through the five-bar gate and on to the unmade lane that led to the paddocks and fields. About a couple of miles, all told. She should be back at the house within an hour, hopefully tired enough to sleep, hopefully having reached a decision.

But by the time she turned for the homeward journey she was wishing she hadn't set out. Despite the punishing physical exercise she was no nearer reaching a decision of any kind. All she wanted was Carlo, and he was like a drug in her veins, bound to lead to her own destruction.

And stamping around the frozen countryside in the middle of the night was futile, definitely one of her sillier moves, and she clambered back over the five-bar gate, disgusted with herself, not taking any care at all. So when she fell it was all her own fault.

That admission, however, added nothing to her comfort. The breath had been knocked out of her body, her hip ached from the way she had landed, and what felt like pounds of snow had got inside her boots.

The ache in her hip and her icy, sodden feet slowed her up. And the enchanted landscape now seemed sinister, the shadows of the trees blacker than they had been before, and she was shuddering with cold, despising herself for her own folly, when the house came into view again.

Most of the lights were on, but her brain was too numbed with the cold and self-inflicted misery to do more than merely register that fact. Because if her wits had been fully functioning she wouldn't have gone rigid with shock when she wearily pushed open the main door and saw Carlo descending the stairs at a gallop, pulling a heavy sweater over the expanse of his naked olive-toned chest.

He jerked to a halt when he saw her and she began to hallucinate, because the look of intense relief in his black eyes couldn't be real, borne out by his grated, 'What the hell do you think you've been doing, woman?'

Self-evident, she would have thought, but she was too weary, too defeated by the sheer force of his unexpected presence to tell him as much. Hands on his jeans-clad hips, he stood looking at her from punishing eyes for a long, breathless second before almost forcibly expelling the air from his lungs and striding over to where she stood, informing her, a cutting edge to his voice, 'I practically turned the house inside out, looking for you. And when I noticed the door wasn't locked and bolted I looked outside.' His eyes withered her. 'A solitary set of footprints, like Orphan Annie. I was on the point of setting out to drag you back.'

'No need. As you see.' Venetia shrugged, despite the soreness of the shoulder that had taken the brunt of her fall, along with her hip. She couldn't remember when she had felt quite this dispirited and weary, but she wasn't going to let him know that. Her chin came up gallantly. 'I don't need a keeper. Perhaps you'll remember that in future.'

If there *was* to be a future for them, she thought disconsolately, the reserve of strength she had called on to help her fight her corner rapidly dissipating beneath the castigation of his sardonically raised brows.

And he told her silkily, 'It's too late to debate that dubious statement. I suggest you get those wet things off and get to bed while I secure the house for what's left of the night.'

Her pale features stony, she looked towards the stairs. Never before had there seemed to be so many. She doubted whether she could put one icily sodden foot in front of the other. Nevertheless, she tried. And heard the sudden grating harshness of his voice.

'You're hurt!'

'No.' Venetia lied because she had to. To confess that the whole of her right side seemed to be aching now, the band of tension-pain around her forehead growing tighter by the second, the biting chill of the cold night still seeping into her bones despite the adequate central heating in the house, would tap the well-spring of self-pity, and she'd probably disgrace herself still further and burst into tears, turn to him for the comfort he wasn't equipped to offer her...

'Then why do you limp so badly?' His voice was brittle with irritation, but there was nothing brittle about the strength of the arms that swept her effortlessly off her feet or the sureness of the stride that carried her up the stairs.

Briefly Venetia tried to summon up the strength to demand to be put down, but gave up the attempt. It was too much effort. Easier to relax in his arms, rest her aching head against the warmth of his sweater-clad chest. Easier, nicer, much, much nicer...

And all too soon he was setting her down on the stool in her bathroom, filling the tub with steaming water, shovelling in great handfuls of scented salts. Only when he knelt at her feet, tugging at the reluctant, soggy boots, did she manage to gather her truant wits.

'Thank you. I can manage,' she said, carefully polite, but he gave her a grim-eyed glare.

'Shut up!' Frowning, he dragged her boots off and then her sodden socks, grabbing a towel from one of the heated rails, rubbing her frozen feet until the circulation came stinging back.

Venetia closed her eyes, trying to hide the sudden brightness of tears. As she watched his downbent head as he cradled her feet in his lap, gently coaxing them back to life, the temptation to run her fingers through his night-dark hair, stroke the thick softness of it, had been almost more than her lowered defences could stand.

But he said, as if she were a child, 'If it hurts, it's getting better.' And that was good, restored a fragment of her tattered self-respect. If he thought she was crying, like a baby, over a transient moment of pain, then she was safe. If he even guessed that her defences were down then she wouldn't be safe at all. Not from him, not from herself.

If she did agree to marry him—and she still couldn't reach a decision, even after hours of soul-searching—then he must never be allowed to know the way she really felt. If he knew she loved him it would only add the pressure of humiliation to all the others inherent in such a perverse situation, make it completely untenable.

Releasing her feet, he stood up, bending over her to remove her anorak, unclipping the waistband of her snow-wettened cords. Venetia's eyes widened in distress, her hands going quickly to push his away.

'I can undress myself,' she stated, her voice emerging on an unfamiliar note of hoarseness. 'I'm not entirely incapable.'

'You are,' he denied, 'or as near as makes no difference. You could barely walk, let alonc gct yourself in and out of the bath unaided.' He eased her hands aside, his long fingers brushing the skin of her tummy as he gripped the waistband more firmly, and her eyes drifted shut as his touch sent incandescent flames through her bloodstream and she moaned with deep shame because all she wanted to do was take his hands between hers and press them against her body.

'Don't pass out on me,' he instructed tersely, obviously mistaking her groan of distress for an indication of how unwell she felt. 'And don't go coy—though you wouldn't, would you?' he growled insultingly. 'You've probably been undressed by a man more times than you've had hot dinners. And don't worry——' he hauled her to her feet, the better to drag the sodden material over her hips '—I'm not about to ravish you. When we make love I'll want you fully fit and capable of joining in the fun.'

'You...!' He infuriated her, disgusted her, but her expression of loathing got no further and ended on a yelp of pain as the heavy fabric dragged against her sore bones. The shock waves of pain made her go giddy, forcing everything else out of her head as she leaned weakly against him, hearing the sudden, sharp intake of his breath.

'How did that happen?'

The skin was slightly broken, already red and inflamed, and Venetia said, feeling a fool, 'I fell off a gate, on to my right side,' and sucked her lower lip between her teeth, not because he was hurting her—he wasn't.

His exploring fingers were impossibly gentle, impossibly arousing too, did he but know it. Her head tipped back dizzily as, his inspection of her hip and thigh completed, he ran his hands over her ribs, beneath her sweater, then, seemingly satisfied, pulled the garment over her head and gave the same gently probing attention to her shoulder.

'No bones broken, at least. You can wiggle your fingers and toes?' he asked impassively, and she nodded, incapable of speech, because he had removed her bra and briefs, and the intimacy of the situation, the tumultuous need he was arousing in her without even trying, had created a vortex of emotion she couldn't handle.

And at least she should be thankful that he had no such problem, she told herself as he scooped her into his arms and lowered her into the water. If he took it into his head to make love to her now, stake his claim, she would be totally unable to stop him. Wouldn't want to stop him, despite her idiotically acquired injuries.

The scented water was blissfully warm and she lay back and let it lap around her chin, summoning up enough spirit to tell him, 'I'm fine now. If I'm not out in half an hour you can come and rescue me.' It was too embarrassing to have him hanging around. Already her breasts were beginning to peak and he would notice, and know, and... 'What the hell do you think you're doing?'

He was stripping off his sweater, and she sat up in a shower of droplets, crossing her arms across her breasts, wincing with the pain of her ill-considered, hasty movement. Her pulse went into overdrive, her heart hammering against her ribs. He was beautiful, the invincible male, radiating power and purpose from the breadth of his thick shoulder muscles to the taut line of his narrow waist. Her eyes followed his every movement as she frantically instilled in herself the need to make him back off even while every feminine instinct within her made her ache to run her fingers over that olive-toned satin skin, intriguingly dusted with crisp dark hair.

If she allowed him to make love to her she would be utterly lost, the question of whether to marry him or not beyond debate, because she would then, irrevocably, belong to him, body, heart and soul. But he informed her tauntingly, 'Don't worry, I'm not about to join you, although, had circumstances been different, nothing would have stopped me. Lie down.' And, at her wide-eyed look of perplexity, he grunted, 'I am going to massage your damaged bits. Nothing more! And I don't particularly want to get my sweater soaked.'

Oh. Of course. He could be quite indifferent to her if he chose. His emotions weren't involved. Unlike her; she only had to be near him to want him quite desperately. Hopelessness welled inside her, but the gentle touch of his hands, moving rhythmically along her injured side, drove everything else out of her head, even despair, and when he asked gruffly, 'What were you doing outside, in this weather, at that time of night?' she had to blink rapidly several times to clear her head.

'Thinking.' Her hand drifted idly through the water. She felt relaxed enough to believe that nothing mattered, nothing at all. 'The house confined me,' she added, drowsy and drowning with the magic of what his touch was doing to her, foolishly regretting that he was sticking both to his word and the 'damaged bits' he had mentioned. 'I thought the fresh air and exercise might clear my head, help me reach a decision.'

'And did it?' He removed his hand from the water and straightened up. 'I would have thought a decision to marry me would have been an easy one to make.'

'Such modesty!' Her voice curled with gentle amusement; she was far too relaxed to snipe at him for such arrogant big-headedness, and when he held out both hands to her, commanding tightly,

'Let's have you out of there, before you get chilled,' she allowed him to help her out, not in the least bit embarrassed by her nakedness now, and huddled blissfully into the huge, warm towel he held out for her, allowing him to pat her dry, feeling pampered and cosseted and, almost, loved.

'Why did you never marry?' she asked cosily, wondering how revealing the answer would be, because there must have been numerous women in the past who would have given rather more than their eye-teeth to get him to change his marital status.

He was very close, drying the hair at the nape of her neck, and she felt his body go still before he answered thickly, a few taut seconds later, 'Because until now I have never felt the need.'

Because of the business? Because of his promise to her father? She didn't know, and probably never would, and suddenly it didn't seem important, not so important, not when his proximity, the warm satin of his skin was so close to her lips, the musky male scent of him overpowering her mind.

She moved her head just the tiny fraction it took to bring her mouth in contact with that tantalising expanse of chest and without her even thinking about it her tongue peeped out between her lips, lapping the hot, musky male skin, and felt the betraying muscular spasm beneath, his flesh responding unmistakably to the eroticism of her mouth. Then she felt his hands on her shoulders, holding her at a tiny, unbridgeable distance as he looked at her and said, 'I know,' his eyes as glittering as his rueful smile as he added huskily, 'But right now you'rc in no fit state. Can you find your own way into a nightdress while I make you a hot drink?'

He didn't even stay long enough to hear her affirmative, and left her wide-eyed, staring at the door he'd closed behind him. If she hadn't known better she would have concluded that, for once, he was afraid of losing control.

However... She dropped the towel and walked through to her bedroom, pulling on the first nightie that came to hand. Her mind was made up. The fiery passions she had schooled right out of her nature had come surging back with a vengeance with his return. And she was going to take the easy way out, stop fighting them. She loved him, she wanted him, and she would marry him.

Tomorrow, and all the rest of her tomorrows, would probably bring regret, she acknowledged as she slipped beneath the duvet. But tonight she wouldn't even think about it, except to allow the tiny chink of hope that he might one day learn to love her, too...

He was wearing his sweater again when he came briskly through the door some minutes later, bearing a glass of hot milk, liberally laced with brandy by the look and smell of it. He set it on the bedside table, his briskness not quite covering the lines of strain around his eyes. And Venetia knew she adored him, always had and always would, and devoured him with her eyes, the bristle of dark stubble decorating his intractable jawline only enhancing his macho appeal.

And she said, her voice much huskier than normal, 'I will marry you, Carlo. Whenever you think fit.' And she felt the full force of those black, fathomless eyes, drowned in them, her own beginning to glitter with inexplicable moistness as he lifted one of her hands, placing his lips in the centre of the palm, the thickness of his lashes hiding his expression as he simply said,

'I promise you'll never regret it, Venetia.'

He would have moved away, but instinct told her she mustn't allow it, not just yet. And her hands clung as she struggled to discover why it was so important to keep him here, just for a short time. And then she knew—how could she have forgotten? But would her word be good enough? It would have to be, wouldn't it? She moistened her lips, her heart clenching as she watched him watch the tiny movement.

'Simon is not my lover——' she said quickly, and would have said a great deal more, reversing his opinion—which went back six whole years—but he cut in, sounding almost uninterested.

'It doesn't matter. It's finished. In the past.' He released his hands from her fevered grip, tucking them firmly beneath the duvet. 'There's precious little time left for sleep—let's take advantage of it, shall we?'

Fine, cut and run, then, she silently told his retreating back, almost laughing aloud. When he eventually made love to her he would have all the proof possible. Simon had never been her lover. No man had. And after that he wouldn't be able to go on believing she was an unprincipled trollop, would he?

CHAPTER SEVEN

VENETIA woke slowly, savouring her body's total relaxation, curling into the warmth of the duvet. And then she remembered and came immediately, vitally awake.

She and Carlo were to be married. The dream that had been born six years ago had come true! She was happier than she felt any human being had a right to be, but wasn't arguing with that!

The cup of tea he had brought her earlier was stone-cold now, and she looked at her watch. Nine-thirty. Water dripping from the eaves bore out what he'd told her—that a rapid thaw had set in—so he had no excuse to cancel the management meeting. He would announce their engagement, no need for her to bother attending, and he would be back before she knew it.

Dropping a light kiss on her forehead, he had gone, looking fantastic in his Italian-styled dark business suit, no sign on his impressive features of a practically sleepless night.

Yawning, she rolled out of bed, determined to attend the management meeting, the latter part of it at least. So she dressed quickly in an understated charcoal-grey suit over a fine-knit light grey sweater.

All her clothes were understated, perhaps too much so? Definitely too much so, she mentally affirmed as she stepped into neat black court shoes. When she and Carlo were married she would allow some of her earlier flamboyance of style back into her life. There was no longer any need to suppress it so ruthlessly, was there?

But the thought of the time when she would be Carlo's wife brought her scurrying activity to a halt, had her staring dreamily into the mirror, not seeing her businesslike reflection at all, her body scarcely able to contain the roiling sensations of delight and wonder. Determination, too. She would do everything in her power to make the marriage work. She wasn't a quitter and he might just find himself learning to love her, despite himself!

Ten minutes later, she was trying to hold the car steady on the slippery, untreated side-roads. They were still treacherous, despite the thaw. Maybe she'd been a fool to get so precipitately out of her warm bed, but it was still her company, even if it was due to shelter securely beneath the Rossi umbrella in the future. Besides, she wanted to be at Carlo's side when he announced their engagement.

Once on the main roads the going was much easier and she was able to put her foot down. It wouldn't be funny if she arrived too late and found the meeting had wound up, Carlo already on his way back to her!

Head office was in Camden Town on the northern side of the capital, and the plane-tree-lined street was relatively quiet; she could hear the rumble of trains on the main line to the Midlands and Scotland behind the large Victorian villas opposite as she got out of the parked car and smoothed the wrinkles out of her skirt.

It wasn't a fashionable part of London, but parking was fairly easy and the converted villa made very adequate offices. Over the past years it had become almost a second home; she had certainly spent more hours here than she had at the house in the country.

As Venetia walked in through the door, stripping off her gloves, Joyce looked up from behind the banked telephones in Reception, surprise all over her comfortable middle-aged face.

'We didn't expect you in today—what with the weather, and everything. The roads must be truly awful round your neck of the woods. How are you, anyway? I didn't have chance to say much to you at the funeral—so many people—but——'

'I'm fine,' Venetia gently cut her short. Joyce was well-meaning, but her garrulity was a byword. Once she got a topic between her teeth she worried it to death, like a dog with a bone, and Venetia didn't want to have to listen to endless condolences. She was just beginning to come to terms, privately and in her own way, with the suddenness, the shock of her loss. 'Is the meeting over?' she followed on smoothly, and Joyce shook her head.

'Not yet. Rumour has it we're going to be a Rossi subsidiary—is there anything in it?'

'There is.' There was no harm in telling the truth, Venetia decided. As soon as the meeting was over the whole company would know. She smiled suddenly, radiantly. Her marriage to Carlo would have that spin-off, and the future of Ross UK would be assured.

The relief was enormous. Until she actually felt the burden being lifted from her shoulders she hadn't realised just what a strain it had all been.

'I'll sit in on the end of the meeting,' she told the receptionist, making for the stairs, and Joyce called after her,

'They're using your office, since it's the largest—oh, and don't let Signor Rossi swindle you out of anything you and your father worked for. I know he's a hunk, and charming with it, but you only have to look at him to know he always comes out right on top of the heap!'

'I won't, believe me!' Venetia carolled back, hugging her precious secret to her. Not that her imminent marriage to Carlo would be a secret much longer. He had probably already announced it. Soon everyone in the building would know. And would probably be just as relieved as she was to learn that the company's future would be assured beneath the umbrella of Rossi International. Part of the family. The breach finally healed.

She was still smiling as she headed for her office, and she was almost there when the door opened and Simon lurched out, banging it behind him. The moment's disappointment that she hadn't, after all, had the opportunity to sit in on the final leg was forgotten when Simon accused, 'Did you know he was going to fire me? Did you?'

He took her arm in a brutal grip, his face white with temper, and Venetia croaked, 'What are you talking about? Who fired you?'

'That damned Italian! Who else?' he snapped bitterly. 'So you didn't know?'

'No.' She shook her head, frowning. Carlo had taken up the reins with a vengeance, and she didn't like it, particularly when he took it upon himself to fire her staff without even the courtesy of a consultation. 'What reason did he give?'

Simon was good at his job, and had taken over the responsibility for buying from her father years ago. His services came expensive, of course—he always insisted he could get better deals if he travelled to their various suppliers, used the personal approach. But in company life, as elsewhere, one got what one paid for, and if Carlo was intent on pruning down expenditure he could have done it without putting Simon out of a job.

Besides, the idea she had had of purchasing all their wines through Rossi would mean that Simon's travelling days, and the expense they incurred, would be more or less over.

'So what was the reason?' she persisted, her brow furrowed, but his hand slid down to hold hers, tugging, his voice terse as he told her,

'I can't talk about it here. Everyone else will be out in a second. Let's go to lunch, get some privacy. He can't fire me without your say-so.'

'He can and he has,' Carlo remarked icily from the doorway. 'Clear your desk, Carew. And you've eaten your last lunch with my fiancée. Understand that, if you value your health.'

Venetia froze. Through the open doorway she could hear the murmur of speculative male voices, and saw Maggie come out, her notebook in her hands, her eyes wide with curiosity as she stepped her way round Carlo's broad back.

Her hand was still in Simon's, she realised, belatedly tugging it away, shivering a little as she watched the way Carlo's eyes narrowed, his mouth hardening as he followed the movement.

'Ah, Venetia . . .' Gordon Manning, the company secretary, was among the first to emerge from the office, a gleam of fatherly approval in his twinkling eyes as he clapped a hand on her shoulder. 'Congratulations. We were all delighted to have the news of your forthcoming marriage. Your father would have been pleased to see the ancient rift between the two families bridged in such a satisfactory way.'

She knew that was the truth, she thought as she accepted the good wishes of all the others. Her father had been deeply gratified when Carlo had appeared all those years ago, his visit an olive-branch in itself. And she knew he had kept in touch, through his phone calls to Carlo, with the Italian branch of the family. Although what had been said between the two men, she had never known. She had made it plain, when he had tried to relay the contents of those phone calls, that she had no interest whatsoever in whatever Carlo Rossi had to say. It had been a defence, of sorts. She had been trying to cut him out of her heart, out of her mind; she hadn't wanted any reminders of him.

Initially, of course, her father had been surprised, to put it mildly, but he had refrained from mentioning Carlo again in her hearing, and for that she had been deeply thankful. They had always been very close; he could, so easily, have dragged the unpalatable truth from her.

She must have been making all the right responses, she realised now. She and Carlo were alone in the corridor and he said grimly, 'I told you to stay at home.'

'So you did,' she agreed absently. 'But the roads weren't that bad. Anyway——' she shrugged such inconsequentialities to one side '—what's all this about giving Simon the boot?'

'It pains you?' he wanted to know, his thumbs hooked into the tiny front pockets of the waistcoat that was an elegant part of his fashionable Italian-designed dark grey suit.

'It dumbfounds me,' she returned crossly, once again suspecting his motives and regretting that she should feel that way. She loved him, she didn't want to think the worst of him, and she heaved a palpable sigh of relief when he slid an arm around her shoulder and drew her into her now deserted office, telling her,

'When you hear my explanation I'm sure you'll agree that I had no other option.' Taking her with him, he sat on the edge of her desk, pulling her between his knees, her thighs firmly anchored by the power of his. 'As you would suspect, I have always kept an eye on my holding in Ross UK, and a little while ago I began to realise that all was not as it should be in the buying department.'

The pressure of his hands on the small of her back increased and she found herself melting forward, her palms going out to rest against his broad chest. Beneath her hands his body felt very hard, and her thighs were burning from the pressure of his, and it was all she could do to concentrate on what he was telling her.

'I asked around and discovered that your friend Simon was lining his pockets at the expense of our company, taking backhanders from a few unscrupulous vineyard owners in return for ordering at over-the-top prices. In my book, that's theft.'

'I can't believe it,' Venetia said, shocked, and showing it. 'He worked so hard for the company, first as father's PA, then mine, fitting in his buying trips somehow. Surely there's some mistake?'

'None at all.' Carlo's eyes slid over her shocked features as he said softly, with a trace of compassion, 'It's not easy to accept betrayal, is it? But, believe me, *carissima*, I have all the proof I need. Your father knew, because I warned him, but, alas, he didn't live long enough to do what was necessary.'

'Then why didn't you come to me with your proof? I should have been told, consulted!' She was having difficulty coming to terms with this. Despite his earlier, obnoxious behaviour, Simon had gone on to prove his worth as friend, adviser and working colleague. She would have vouched for his integrity without even having to think about it, while all the time—according to

Carlo—he had been supporting a luxurious lifestyle at the company's expense.

It took a lot of getting used to and, frowning, she bit out, 'Why was I the last to know?'

'Hush...' He laid a finger on her lips, rubbing gently, and she went soft inside, his touch a magical chemical injected into her bloodstream. And his black eyes were warm as he told her, 'With the shock of your father's sudden death you had enough to contend with. You must learn to allow me, as your future husband, to look after your interests.' His finger was playing an erotic game with her parted, lush mouth, dipping slowly into each corner with sensual expertise, his head lowering, coming closer, so that her slanting, slumbrous eyes took in each individual gold-tipped black lash, the glint of leashed passion in the black, black eyes.

And then his mouth took hers, his tongue delving tantalisingly into her sweet moistness as his hands went to her quivering flanks, pulling her closer between the hard intimacy of his parted thighs, and she fitted her hips into his with an instinctive feminine response, her hands moving feverishly beneath his jacket in a wild need to know every inch of his body...

And when at last he broke the kiss she was trembling with uncontrollable need, a need echoed in the rawness of his voice as he told her, 'I'm glad you came after all. I'd meant to phone you, but this is better.' He stood up, supporting her by her elbows as she sagged against him, her knees too weak to hold her slight weight. His mouth took on a wry slant. 'Unfortunately, I had an urgent summons back to head office in Rome. It came under an hour ago and there's nothing I can do to avoid it. I can't see myself getting back to you in anything under a week.'

'Oh, hell!' Half an hour ago everything had seemed perfect. Well, almost, given the fact she had just agreed to marry a man who didn't yet know he was going to learn to love her! And now he was calmly walking away because business would always come first with him. Added to which, she had just learned that an employee she would have trusted with the last breath in her body had turned out to be a thieving skunk.

And as she wasn't stupid enough to believe that anything she could say would dissuade Carlo from attending to his paramount business concerns, she said, more waspishly than she had intended, disappointment making her mouth take on a sulky pout, 'Are you quite sure you're right about Simon? Couldn't you be putting two and two together and coming up with five—just because you might be a tiny bit jealous?'

It did make a kind of sense, in the circumstances. Carlo believed that she and Simon had been lovers for years—even continuing their supposed affair after he'd married Angie, something she herself had stupidly led him to believe. So he might have uncovered the fact that Simon had made a couple of dubious deals, nothing really dishonest, but not very ethical, and used his knowledge to punish the other man in the most devastating way he could.

'Do you think so little of my integrity?' Hard hands on her shoulders thrust her away, and she tilted her head and saw anger whiten his face. And his black eyes withered her, his lips barely moving as he ground out, 'Or does he still mean so much to you that you would fight his corner no matter what he'd done?'

Shaken, Venetia closed her eyes, her voice a bare whisper as she said, 'I'm sorry. I didn't intend you to take it that way.' She was bitterly disappointed because he was leaving, putting business first, and had taken it out on him, she acknowledged miserably.

'Then tell me how I was supposed to take such a staunch defence?' he invited slightly more equably, as if he regretted the outburst and was forcing control. 'It was hardly flattering.'

Venetia shrugged unhappily. How could she explain the childish confusion of her feelings without betraying how much she adored him, how the week he had said he would be away would seem like an eternity? Their relationship wasn't ready for such an admission. He would find it embarrassing, or amusing. She didn't know which would be worse, and she mumbled with some truth, 'I can't get over the shock. Hearing that someone you trusted implicitly has been diddling you left, right and centre can hurt.'

'I can imagine.' His beautiful mouth slanted wryly. 'However, I refuse to spend what little time we have at our disposal discussing your precious Simon. You're going to have to come to terms with his double-dealing in your own way, in your own time, and reach some sensible conclusions. And that's the last I want to hear on the subject.'

He reached his superbly styled silk and mohair over-coat from the hatstand and draped it over his shoulders. It made him look even more powerful, rakish, part of another world. Never before had he seemed so dark, so foreign. And he was saying, 'I'm taking you to lunch. There's just enough time before I need to leave for the airport.' He held out his hand and she took it happily. The smile he gave her was dazzling, enfolding her in warmth.

He was obviously more than willing to put their spat over Simon's dismissal behind them. And so was she.

She wished she'd made more of a determined effort to make him believe the truth about her relationship with the other man. But now was definitely not the time to bring the subject up. He had categorically stated that he didn't want to hear Simon's name mentioned one more time, and he might even see her attempted clarification as a belated try at dissociating herself from a man who carried the taint of proven criminal activities.

So she would leave it, confident in the knowledge that sooner or later he would discover the truth for himself. Later now, rather than sooner, she mourned inwardly, trying not to look as disconsolate as she felt.

The precious hour with him sped by far more quickly than she liked. She couldn't bear to be apart from him, she admitted as she made a gallant pretence of enjoying the superb food in the nearby restaurant. The discovery of small but exclusive eating-houses tucked away in the most unlikely corners of London was one of the capital's most endearing surprises. She and her father had happened across this one a couple of years ago and she was glad they had, because it meant that the time at Carlo's disposal hadn't been eroded by having to travel into the centre.

'There's so much to talk over, and not much time.' Black eyes smiled into hers as the waiter brought their mineral water to the table and went away with their order. Venetia caught her lower lip between her teeth. When he smiled at her that way her bones melted and her brain turned to mush and she could almost believe she meant something to him, something special, and quite separate from mere animal desire and a businessman's need to tidy up loose ends.

'So—first things first.' His eyes held hers, glimmers of devilment glinting in the black depths, disarming her utterly. 'We will marry in three weeks' time. I think a simple civil ceremony would be best, considering your recent bereavement, don't you?' And, not giving her time to state any opinion, 'You can leave that side of it to me; all you need to do is choose something pretty to wear to our wedding and pack for our honeymoon. Which, by the way——' he leaned back as the waiter brought their first course, his eyes never leaving her face as he delivered '—we shall spend at my villa in Sardinia.'

Her slanting eyes narrowed beneath her sudden frown. Carlo picked up his fork, one brow lifting.

'You have objections? Would you prefer somewhere else?'

'No, of course not.' She hesitated. 'It's just that I know so little of you, of your life. I had no idea you had a villa in Sardinia, that's all.'

She picked up her own fork and began to eat, surprised all at once by the enigma of him. And the deep huskiness of his voice surprised her all over again, forcing her slanting eyes to lock with his as he told her, 'My life is an open book. You only have to ask, *cara*, and all will be revealed. However——' he dazzled her all over again with the brilliance of his smile '—I think you and I will derive a great deal of pleasure in the exercise of finding out all there is to know about each other.'

His words, the tone of his voice, conjured enough erotic mind pictures to make her blush—which had been his intention, no doubt. And while she was still trying to recover her composure, he advised, 'Don't worry about the business—everything's in hand—and don't even think of selling the house. As we shall spend part of each year in England, it will be convenient to have it as a base. And if you're worried about leaving it empty for long stretches of time, why don't you consider keeping Potty on to housekeep in our absence? And to go one step further...' He tipped his head on one side, considering her. 'You tell me that Potty feels responsible for her sister—Enid, isn't it? That she feels guilty because she doesn't see her as often as she believes she ought. So why not get a couple of rooms converted back at the house and have Enid move in? That way we would be killing two birds with one stone—providing Potty with employment, the house with a sitter, and stifling Enid's grumbles about imagined neglect at source. Think about it.'

'I will.' And she would. But not now. Right now, despite her better judgement, she had to know, 'Will you miss me?' and cursed herself for the yearning she clearly detected in her own voice, for the tiny betrayal that might give him insight into the way she really felt about him. And cursed herself afresh for the soaring lilt of joy he gave her when he replied in the affirmative, his voice as soft and tender as his smile, making her believe just for a heady moment that he meant it.

And she went on foolishly believing it until she spoiled everything when, as the waiter came back to clear their plates, she smiled at him, spoke to him by name. Carlo said coldly, 'You obviously make a habit of coming here. I take it this is the "usual place" where you and Simon indulge in long, intimate lunches? A pity. I had been enjoying myself immensely until now.'

And as she opened her mouth to deny that she had ever been here with Simon, only with her father, he cut in brutally, 'Don't let's make an issue of it. I'm quite prepared to forget the bastard ever existed, if you are.' He shot a cool glance at his wristwatch. 'As my wife, you will have no past, only a future. And now you will have to excuse me.'

He pushed himself back from the table and beckoned for the bill, waving away the waiter who had unwittingly been the cause of the upset and was now hovering uncertainly with their main course. And Venetia flashed, 'Just like that! You get a foul idea into your head and you won't let it go; well, I'm sorry for you.' Her cheeks flaming, she gathered her handbag and gloves, her eyes hating him across the small table. So much for those brief moments of shared closeness, the rare tenderness, fragile moments so easily shattered by one ill-chosen word. Could a future with him be anything other than purgatory? Her mouth went firm, her colour dying away as she met his eyes and told him, 'Before we go any further I have to tell you that you won't be getting a zombie for a wife—a creature with no past, I think you said. No mind of her own. Only a future spent dancing to your changeable tunes.' Her voice shook and she took a moment to control it, walking ahead of him to the pavement, turning then, her face pale as she said, 'I do have some pride. I don't think the sort of future you have in mind for us is something I can handle.'

'You will handle it beautifully.' He looked at her, his expression unreadable. 'And I know exactly what I shall be getting as a wife.' He took her arm, propelling her rapidly back towards the office, leaving her bereft of breath, lost for an answer as he added coolly, 'And if I can handle that, then so can you.'

CHAPTER EIGHT

CARLO'S phone call came as Venetia was getting ready for bed, and the gloom of her near-decision to back out of the marriage was spirited away by the sheer magic of his voice. And when his flowers arrived the next morning she had to face the fact that she would always be a sucker as far as he was concerned.

She couldn't wait to have him back and, from the message on the card that accompanied the flowers, he couldn't wait either. But she would have plenty to do in the interim to keep her mind from brooding over his absence, missing him.

And so it proved. Potty, when she finally made it back to the house, was utterly delighted by the news of the wedding and almost as pleased with the idea of her staying on as housekeeper in their absence, with Enid installed in her own suite of rooms.

'She won't mind giving up her independence, her own home?' Venetia asked, wondering if Carlo could possibly be missing her as much as she was missing him.

'She'll be glad to get shot of the responsibility. And if she's here I won't have to feel guilty about not traipsing over to visit her as often as she thinks I should. I thought I'd go mad, shut up with her in the middle of a snow-storm! At least if we're under the same roof she'll be happy enough if I pop in for ten minutes half a dozen times a day! And what are you going to wear for your wedding? That's the most important thing at the moment. And I know you said it would be a quiet affair, but wild horses won't keep me away. So be warned!'

'I wouldn't dream of getting married without you there to wish me well.' Impulsively Venetia flung her arms around the older woman. 'You're the next best thing to a mother, so don't you ever forget it!'

'Get along with you!' Potty chided, but her eyes were bright with tears. So were Venetia's, for that matter, so they did the sensible thing and settled themselves in the cosy kitchen to share a pot of tea and discuss the intriguing topic of a trousseau.

The snow disappeared almost as quickly as it had fallen. Winter's last fling had turned into a tentative spring practically overnight, and Venetia, vowing to keep busy to prevent herself pining over Carlo, decided to put in a full day at work, sandwiching a trip into town for shopping at Harrods in between being briefed by her managers on Carlo's ideas for the rationalisation of the company.

Gossip about Simon's dismissal was rife among the staff, but Venetia refused to be drawn into any discussion on the subject. His betrayal still hurt because, after a bad beginning, they had become friends. She couldn't understand how he could have cheated them, especially her father, who had always held him in high esteem.

The arrival of Roberto Torino, Carlo's steely-eyed company solicitor, had her closeted all day with him and their own solicitor, working out the finer details of the coming merger. At six-thirty they called it a day with Venetia declining Signor Torino's invitation to dinner with as much grace as she could summon.

The day had been long, successful, but wearisome, and the last thing she wanted to do was make small talk over dinner. Carlo had been gone for four days now and all she wanted to do was have an early night, dream of him, and when the morning came there would only be another three days to get through before she saw him again. One way or another she was going to make their marriage work, earn his respect and love. As she hadn't the strength of will necessary to cut him totally out of her life, then she didn't have any other option.

It was Potty's night for bingo in the village hall, and the house was silent as she let herself in and uninterestedly read the note the housekeeper had left on a hall table. The information that there was a venison casserole in the warming oven of the Aga was not something she was particularly interested to hear. With Carlo away, she felt edgy, unsure of him and, even if she was loath to admit it, a little afraid of their future, of the pain it could bring.

But maybe he would phone again tonight; hearing his warm, sexy voice always made her feel better, more confident of the future. Last night he had missed, which was probably why she was beginning to feel as if she were walking on pins.

Besides, he was a busy man. His business interests were spread worldwide, and, apparently, he insisted on keeping his fingers on the pulse of every last one of them, making all the decisions, taking most of the strain.

He had gone back to his Italian headquarters to answer an urgent summons and put in as much work as he could, leaving him free to spend their honeymoon in Sardinia, where work would be the last thing either of them would be thinking of, she told herself as she marched upstairs to strip off her suit and take a shower. So it was hardly surprising if he didn't find time to phone her every single night. So there was no reason at all why she should feel uneasy.

Half an hour later, showered and dressed for comfort in a turquoise silk housecoat that deepened the colour of her eyes to sapphire, she wandered downstairs. She would curl up in front of the small sitting-room fire with some of that casserole and watch a little television. She would probably be in bed by the time Potty returned by taxi at around eleven. More relaxed now, she was able to contemplate an early night with some enthusiasm.

In the warm little sitting-room she switched on the two table lamps with old gold shades and doused the main light. The flickering firelight, the glow from the lamps, touched the pale oak panelling with loving fingers, and Venetia felt sadness engulf her, the sudden lump in her throat painful and depressing.

This, of all the beautiful rooms in the house, had been her and her father's favourite. They had spent so many happy, relaxing hours here, listening to music, playing chess or simply talking. She couldn't believe he would never smile at her again from his squashy old armchair at the side of the hearth, invite her to tell him all about her day.

So when she heard the peal of the doorbell she was almost stupidly thankful. Any company would ease this grieving sense of loneliness, all the more intense because Carlo was away. When they were together the atmosphere was too intense to allow depression a look in.

And, quite regardless of the fact that she wasn't dressed for receiving visitors, she dragged the main door open, found Carlo on the doorstep, grinned at him stupidly for one breathless moment, then threw herself into his arms, her joy at seeing him uncontainable.

'Hey!' He sounded breathless, too, as he broke away from her frantic rain of kisses, unclasping her hands from around his neck and holding them firmly between his, a wry smile on his sensuous mouth. 'Don't I get further than the doorstep before I'm leapt on?'

'No.' She smiled up at him, her eyes quite wicked. The poised, ultra-controlled woman she had trained herself to become had gone missing. And she didn't even care! Her passionate nature was seeing the light of day once more, and Venetia was revelling in it. 'You didn't phone last night. I thought you'd forgotten me—oh, Carlo, you can't begin to imagine how I've missed you!'

Her fingers were twining with his, her slender, silk-wrapped body straining closer to the dark warmth of his. She couldn't get close enough, but when he said thickly, 'I will never forget you, you can count on that,' warmth flooded her heart and the first real, not to be doubted ray of hope entered her soul.

'When did you arrive back in England?' she asked, breathless with the discovery she had made, and he told her,

'About an hour and a half ago. I drove straight from the airport.'

'You should have let me know,' she chided gently. 'I might not have been available.' She brought her hands up, her fingertips touching his lips, lips that scarcely moved as he said,

'For me, you will always be available, *cara*. I shall demand no less.'

A tiny, involuntary shiver rippled down her spine. The intensity of his desire became more apparent at every encounter; could it be translated into something deeper, longer-lasting? Or would it burn itself out, leaving nothing behind but the sour taste of regret?

'Do we have to conduct our reunion on the doorstep, *cara*? You are getting cold, I think.'

'I'm sorry,' she said, her voice muffled against the hard wall of his chest, and made to draw him inside, out of the darkness and into the light, but the headlamps of an approaching car swept over them, tyres crunching on the gravel, bringing a frown to mar the smooth perfection of her forehead.

It was too early for Potty's taxi to be bringing her home—unless she had been taken ill. The thought took hold of her by the throat, frightening her, so when Simon slid out of the car she experienced nothing but relief.

She heard Carlo say something—probably obscene—in Italian as he stepped further over the portal, into the hall. He seemed larger than life, a strangely menacing shadow among the somewhat nebulous tones of light and shade in the dimly lit hall.

But Venetia was too relieved that her fear that dear old Potty had been taken ill at bingo had been completely unfounded to spare more than a fleeting frown for Carlo's sombre withdrawal.

Of course he wouldn't be pleased to have their privacy invaded—and by Simon, of all people. Neither was she, come to that, especially as he had been cheating the company that had provided him with well-paid, secure employment for so many years.

Nevertheless, a basic if grudging politeness demanded that she step forwards into the ring of light shed by the security lamps and ask, with the inbred courtesy which disguised her annoyance and distaste, 'Simon—what can I do for you?' And she was totally unprepared for the way he looked, his face almost ashen, scored by lines that hadn't been there the last time she'd seen him, or for the way he said rawly,

'You know damn well what you can do for me, Venny!' And strode jerkily on up the steps, gathering her to him as he went, hustling her into the hall and slamming the door closed behind them.

And only then, into the still, shadowy silence, did Carlo speak.

'You've got five seconds to state your business, Carew. Five seconds between you and a prosecution, instead of a straightforward firing.'

There was no heat in his tone, nothing but a cool and deadly intent, and Venetia shuddered, almost, but not quite, feeling sorry for the younger man, because, after all, he deserved anything Carlo cared to throw at him.

She could feel Simon psyching himself up to stand his shaky piece of ground, feel it in the way his arm tightened around her waist, in the stiff rigidity of his body, so close to her own. And if he did attempt to defy Carlo then he would bring an avalanche of cold retribution down on his head.

Venetia couldn't allow that to happen. Somehow she had to smooth things over. She wouldn't let further rancour between these two ruin this precious reunion or shatter the fragile beginnings of a real and worthwhile relationship. But she would have to tread carefully.

So she asked, her tone cool as ice, 'Simon, can what you've come to say be said in five minutes?' and, at his terse nod, gave Carlo a swift, conciliatory glance, received the black ferocity of his eyes in recompense, and stamped firmly on the feeling that she had just made one hell of a mistake.

This was her home, and, if she couldn't give five minutes of her time to a one-time friend and employee without Carlo Rossi looking at her as if he were privately measuring her for a pair of cement boots, then she might just as well give up all hope of a partnership of equals and take a crash course in how to be a doormat.

She would explain everything later, she thought, watching her fiancé's broad back disappear through the door to the kitchen regions. Tell him that she had wanted to avoid a possibly violent confrontation—something which could well have happened if Simon had been forcibly shown the door without having said what he had come to say. Explain, too, about the way she instinctively knew that her father would have wanted her to try to get to the bottom of it all, find out why a valued employee had suddenly decided to cheat...

'Five minutes,' she reiterated as she led Simon to the study. 'If you've come to ask for your job back, then I'm afraid it's not up to me, so you'll be wasting your time. As you know, we are merging with Rossi, and, while it's good for the company, it leaves me without my former autonomy. Besides——' she took her father's chair behind the big desk, gesturing him to take the smaller one on the other side '—you don't deserve any concessions, in the circumstances. I always believed you could be trusted.'

'You don't understand; I don't want my job back.' Simon shot her an impatient look beneath his brows. But his face had turned a surly red. 'Sure, I took a few backhanders. I looked on them as part of the job—perks, if you like. And Angie's got expensive tastes.'

Which didn't excuse a damn thing, Venetia thought, hardening her heart. She should have let Carlo throw him off the premises.

'You've hardly been married for five minutes,' she reminded him tartly. 'So don't heap the blame on Angie. Besides, she must earn enough to satisfy the most expensive tastes.'

She was beginning to wish she'd refused to let him over the doorstep. He had openly admitted doing the company down, and he wasn't stupid enough to really believe that what he had done came within the category of legitimate perks. In putting the blame on Angie he had opened her eyes to the unpleasant side of his character, the side she had gradually forgotten during the past few years when he had set out to ingratiate himself.

But Simon shook his head, repeating, 'You don't understand. What Angie earns is hers and what I earn is hers. That's the way she sees it, anyway. And, however much there is, it isn't enough.' He got to his feet, restlessly pacing the room, his hands in his trouser pockets, his shoulders high with tension. 'I'm divorcing her. I should never have married her. It was the oldest trick in the book. "Darling, I'm pregnant, I don't know how it happened. My whole career is ruined—so what are you going to do about it?"' he mimicked cruelly. 'Needless to say, it was all a false alarm. Or a downright lie. She needed a husband to provide her with everything she believes she has a right to. What's more, she's rapidly approaching her sell-by date; she needed someone to keep her, so she tricked me into marriage.'

'I'm sorry,' Venetia said stiltedly, getting to her feet.

His marital difficulties were his own affair and in no way excused his dishonesty. He had probably been taking bribes for years before he had even met his wife. When she remembered how much her father had trusted him she felt ill with pent-up anger.

'Don't be.' Simon had obviously misread her, catching hold of her shoulders as she was on her way to the door ready to show him out, swinging her round. 'My marriage was a dreadful mistake,' he said thickly. 'You're the only woman I've ever loved. And I don't want my job back—that's not the reason I'm here. I wouldn't work for Rossi if he paid me in diamond-studded gold bars.'

His face had turned dull red and his eyes were hot, and Venetia said coldly, 'Please let me go.'

'You don't mean that—you know you don't!' His hands slid down to her waist, pulling her closer. He was breathing hard and, the more she tried to free herself, the tighter his hold on her became, and Venetia was beginning to be frightened now because he was obviously sexually aroused, and he was muttering against her ear, his voice slurred, as if he'd been drinking heavily, 'We wanted each other, years ago. But you were a tease and I rushed you. You seemed ripe for the plucking. I forgot how young you were until you threatened to lose me my job. Remember? So I backed off. But I never stopped wanting you. Never.'

He disgusted her, Venetia thought sickly, pounding uselessly against his chest. She didn't know how she had got herself into this situation, and trying to fight off his superior strength wasn't the way to handle it, she decided distraughtly.

If she screamed loudly enough to alert Carlo, he would come to her rescue—but at what price? The result would be mayhem and, more importantly as far as she was concerned, the situation might only reinforce his belief that she and Simon had been lovers for years, that the other man was only trying to take what was his, that she had been responsible for what was happening, that she had asked for it.

Somehow, she had to defuse the situation. Twisting her head away from his marauding mouth, she said as calmly as she could, 'This isn't getting us anywhere, I don't want to fight you, so why don't you tell me why you came, if it wasn't to ask for your job back? I'm listening.'

Her heart was pounding against her ribs and she felt sick with frightened disgust. But her pacifying words seemed to have done the trick because his hold on her slackened fractionally and he stopped trying to kiss her and said, 'I know you don't want to fight me, Venny. You can't fool me. I know all about the smouldering volcano under that ice-maiden image you've affected over the past few years. I was there when it gave the first signs of erupting, remember? And who did you come to when you wanted to learn all there was to know about the family business? Who did you turn to when your father died? But you've got a point...' He tilted back his head, his smile oily. 'I haven't properly explained myself. Listen, I've already told you I intend to get a divorce. Marry me, Venny; forget Rossi. I know why you agreed to marry him—to secure the company's future. When he announced your engagement at that meeting that much came over, loud and clear. Well, sod the company! Why should you sacrifice yourself like that?'

His hands were stroking her back, rubbing the silk against her bare flesh, but Venetia was too busy thinking about what he'd said to notice. Had Carlo really implied, at that management meeting, that they were marrying for the sake of the company—and no other reason? Even though it was the truth, it hurt her to know he had spelled it out so publicly. And, what was even worse, it had given Simon the excuse for his odious suggestions.

Carefully, she extricated herself from his roaming hands and was inutterably relieved when he allowed her to step back a pace, but he was telling her, his rapid words hardly impinging now, 'Sell your shares in the company to Rossi—that's all he's interested in anyway—and get out. Get rid of this great mausoleum, too. And we'll go away together, just you and I. Just think about it—neither of us would ever have to work again; we could lie in the sun all day and make love all night. You'd never regret it, I promise.'

She barely registered anything else that Simon said, and was trying to work out how she could get him to quietly leave without causing the type of scene that would bring Carlo running, when a cold voice spoke from the shadowed doorway, slicing through the torrid atmosphere like a steel blade.

'I, too, can make promises. And I give you my assurance that if you don't leave at once, Carew, the only thing you'll see for the next six months is the inside of a hospital ward.'

How long had he been standing there? How much had he heard?

Venetia froze, her blood turning to ice. She inched round slowly. Carlo didn't move. He didn't need to. His threat was impressive, something no sane man would disregard. And Simon wasn't completely crazy, although, listening to his rabid suggestions, she had begun to think he must be. But he couldn't be, because he didn't say a word, just scuttled out of the room, giving the dark, flint-eyed Italian as wide a berth as was possible.

And then there was nothing but a thick silence. Venetia flicked her tongue over her lips but she couldn't think of a thing to say. If she stumbled verbally to her own defence then Carlo would know that something had been going on. He wasn't at all sure of her innocence where Simon was concerned to believe her above suspicion.

It all depended upon how much he had heard, the way he had translated Simon's ravings, and she practically sagged with relief when Carlo advanced further into the room, his voice completely matter-of-fact as he told her, 'He'd had far more than the five minutes you granted him. And I'm quite sure you can't have wanted to prolong your final meeting.' He sauntered over to stand behind her father's desk, his long fingers idly moving the papers spread across the surface, his voice almost flat as he stated, 'I can understand that anything he had to say to you can only have been an embarrassment.'

Venetia caught at that, apprehension making her mouth go dry as she repeated huskily, 'Embarrassment?' Did that mean he had overheard the stupid things Simon had said? Was she going to have to launch into some kind of defence, make excuses that would sound lame at best; reinforce those suspicions he harboured concerning her ongoing relationship with the other man?

But Carlo merely said, 'How else could you feel, having to hold any kind of conversation with a man who has proved himself to be little better than a common thief? And, what is worse, a traitor to yourself and, before you, to your father.' One dark brow rose significantly and, only too happy to have that uncomplicated interpretation, Venetia grabbed at it, her lush mouth curving in a smile of pure relief.

'Absolutely!' And then, because she didn't want to talk about Simon any more, or even think of him, she swished her way across the room and tucked her arm through Carlo's, her slanting eyes warm as she suggested, 'Come on through to the sitting-room. We can eat there. Potty's left a casserole.'

She badly wanted to kiss him, to feel those strong arms around her again. But he didn't look approachable, perhaps not in the mood for all the pent-up passion she was aching to offer. Not in the mood to share the simple pleasures of a meal in the firelight and a shared bottle of wine, because he said softly, 'I think not. I made coffee while I was waiting for you to say your farewells to Carew. But don't let me stop you.'

His voice was like silk, but his eyes were black ice. Venetia shivered—she couldn't help it—her teeth clamping down hard on her lower lip as he gave her a slight, urbane smile and excused himself, 'I didn't have time to tell you, but I decided it would be best if I booked into a hotel until the wedding. Dine with me tomorrow—we have several arrangements to discuss.'

'The wedding? Or the merger?' she asked with chilling sarcasm. He was leaving, staying at a hotel. And it hurt. Just when she believed they were growing closer, he backed off. And she didn't know why.

Obviously he hadn't arrived on the scene in time to see her apparently wrapped in Simon's arms, or heard the damning rubbish the other man had been spouting—otherwise she would have known about it, and how!

So that couldn't be the cause of his cool withdrawal, and if the words she had flung at him echoed her doubts, held a tinge of bitterness, she couldn't help it. And, as if her distress had cut through all that terrifying remoteness, he took her hand, dipped his dark head, and planted a light kiss in her palm, another on the inner curve of her wrist, his tone lighter now as he taunted, 'Our wedding, of course. The merger can look after itself. Now, sleep well, *carissima*, and be sure you dream of me.'

CHAPTER NINE

THE last three weeks had passed like a dream, and Venetia had the feeling that she didn't really exist at all, that reality had receded beyond recall.

Even her brand new husband seemed more like a figment of her imagination than warm flesh and blood, she thought bemusedly, glancing at him as the private Rossi jet prepared to land at Alghero airport. Beneath them, the blue Mediterranean crinkled against the white beaches of northern Sardinia, and that only served to add to the illusion of being out of time and out of place.

His face looked bloodless beneath the olive tones of his skin and his mouth was grim. She had barely been able to coax the smallest smile from him since the quiet civil ceremony that had joined them as man and wife such a few short hours ago.

But he had worked so very hard, she excused, insisting on personally visiting every one of the Ross UK branches scattered all over Britain. She had hardly seen him during the weeks prior to the wedding, although he had phoned every night, his dark, seductive voice making her go weak with love for him.

It had been during those weeks that the sense of unreality had set in, she decided, gripping the sides of her luxurious seat as the jet touched down. It had hardly seemed credible that the man she had loved with such wild passion all those years ago had re-entered her life like a violent explosion, claiming her, taking her over, altering everything. Too much happiness had addled her brain, made her weak and will-less, transforming her back into the dreamy wanton she had become when she had first set eyes on him six years ago.

Not that she was fighting it, she thought, a tiny smile curving the lush fullness of her coral-tinted lips as her pale, slanting black-fringed eyes lingered on the dark physical perfection of her husband.

She knew now why she had been able to throw herself into her work so single-mindedly, never dating, rarely socialising. She had been in limbo, her heart and soul pledged to the only man she could ever love, although she hadn't seen it that way, of course, not then. Now she knew it for the truth it was and, in a strange way, she was in limbo again. Waiting. Waiting. And she said huskily, 'How far is it to your villa? How long will it take?' The waiting would soon be over. Soon they would be man and wife in the fullest sense of the word. Her beloved Carlo would make her whole, a complete woman, because she was the other half of him. No more limbo, just full and glorious ecstatic reality. And out of that shared ecstasy, love would eventually grow for him. She would make it grow. She had witnessed its fragile beginnings around the time of the announcement of their marriage. Hadn't she?

'It's about a twenty-minute drive. Luigi will meet us with the car.'

Carlo was busy stacking papers back into his briefcase. He had seemed preoccupied with them during the flight—well, as far as she knew. She had fallen asleep after they'd been airborne for about an hour, tiredness overcoming her because she'd hardly slept a wink last night, her mind churning with thoughts of the day ahead. Her wedding day.

'And then you will be able to relax,' he went on, closing the briefcase with a snap and unbuckling his seatbelt as the plane came to a halt. 'Rosa will settle you in and bring you a tray of tea and you can laze around for an hour or so before dinner.'

Rosa? Her long eyes questioned him briefly as she stood up and smoothed the wrinkles out of the skirt of the suit she'd been married in. But he wasn't looking at her, and the radiance of his smile was for the pert and attractive flight attendant who appeared to help them leave the plane. Venetia held her tongue. It wasn't the right time to ask why he shouldn't want to be the one to settle her in.

On the drive to the airport, back in Britain, he had explained that Rosa and Luigi looked after the family holiday villa between them. Native Sards, they had a fierce sense of loyalty, and she, Venetia, would find her every wish attended to because she was his wife, despite the language barrier which meant that they would be unable to communicate verbally. And she brought this up now, as they were driving away from the airport environs.

'I'm going to have to learn the language, aren't I?' She smiled at the back of Luigi's head. A short, stocky man of middle years, he had proffered an effusive but unintelligible greeting. His brown eyes had twinkled with easygoing good humour and she had instinctively wanted to communicate. At her side, Carlo shrugged and crossed one elegantly clothed leg over the other.

'If you really feel you should.' He didn't sound wildly interested and Venetia explained,

'Of course I should. Italian is the language of my roots, after all. And when I meet your family it would be handy if I could speak to them!' She heard the tinge of sarcasm in her voice and wondered what had got into her. She and Carlo were at the very beginning of their honeymoon, so why should she snipe at him for what had been, after all, a perfectly reasonable reply to her comment?

'Your roots?' He took her up, looking straight ahead at nothing with bored, brooding eyes. 'Your mother was English.'

'Welsh, actually,' Venetia corrected, a tiny frown between her eyes, because this wasn't at all the way she had imagined they would be together.

But he didn't seem to have heard her. He didn't comment, merely added suavely, 'And my family, all of whom you will meet when we return to the mainland, are cosmopolitan enough to speak your own language. And as for Luigi and Rosa, their dialect is Catalan—the Sards jealously maintain their own language, which has many different dialects. However——' he looked at her, his eyes dark and oblique '—they all speak Italian—with an admirable purity. Rosa might be willing to teach you a little.'

His minimal shrug and the way he turned his head to stare out of the window at his side told her that he wasn't interested either way, and the pout of her luscious mouth would have told him, had he been looking her way, that his willingness to offload her on to his housekeeper wasn't exactly what she had had in mind for their honeymoon!

Turning her head, she too stared out of the window, but saw absolutely nothing of the passing scenery because her eyes were blurred with tears. Far from behaving like a lover, eager to begin his life with the woman he had married only half a day ago, he was acting as if she actually bored him! Could he be bored with her already? Was that the problem? There were people who lost interest in the thing they wanted the moment they possessed it. Was he one of them?

He was confusing her, making her feel miserable and tense, and it was just crazy! Biting down hard on the corner of her wide lower lip, she managed to stifle a sob at birth, but had to struggle to pull herself together as Luigi pulled the limousine up in front of what had to be Carlo's villa.

And somehow she was able to act normally, even smile, as the chauffeur came round to open the door on her side. The warmth and sunlight helped, of course—so different from the climate back home—and the villa looked inviting.

It was long and low, painted in earth tones, roofed with red tiles, and behind the arcaded façade she glimpsed dozens of tiny windows. And behind the house and around it, as far as the eye could see, the primitive, rugged landscape was colourful with spring flowers.

It was remote, but beautiful, the perfect spot for a honeymoon. Only hers wasn't shaping up the way she had expected it to, she thought broodingly as Carlo cupped his hand beneath her elbow and began to urge her forward, leaving Luigi to deal with the luggage.

He wasn't really touching her; his fingers were merely grazing the soft cream fabric of her sleeve in a token gesture, a politeness he would have shown to any member of her sex. She shivered forlornly. Suddenly, she felt utterly alone.

Which was pretty damn stupid of her, she told herself firmly, and made herself look up at him, made herself smile.

'I know I'm going to love it here. It's beautiful—and the air's so soft and warm. Lovely!'

'Indeed.' His eyes were blank as they met hers briefly and his voice was almost insultingly polite as he told her, 'This is perhaps the best time of year. Later, in the height of the summer, it can become too hot, the towns too crowded. Used as you are to the English climate——'

'Do we have to talk about the bloody weather?' Venetia dug her heels in, her face going red. She didn't understand what was going on, why he had to be so hatefully remote; she only knew that his attitude distressed her unbearably. 'Don't you think it's a little early in our married life to have to resort to such banalities?'

'I thought, wrongly, apparently, that you might be interested.' A flicker of something that could have been amusement softened the hard lines of his mouth for a moment, and Venetia gave him a suspicious glare, tilting her head, the rich blackness of her hair gleaming like burnished silk in the sunlight as his grip on her arm tightened, pushing her onwards.

Luigi had caught them up, cases dangling from both arms, so now wasn't the time to indulge in a quarrel. Not that she wanted to quarrel with him—far from it. She wanted, needed him to hold her in his arms, tell her he still wanted her. And, later, he would, of course he would, she reminded herself, trying to feel blithe about it and almost succeeding as he led her over the portal into a cool, dim hall.

And the short round woman who moved forwards to greet them just had to be Rosa. She was smiling all over her wrinkled face and wisps of greying hair were escaping from the would-be severity of her bun, and Carlo's smile was full of genuine warmth and affection as he greeted her and made the necessary introductions. Introductions which had Venetia mentally renewing her vow to learn her husband's language. But that happy contemplation was shattered when Carlo told her smoothly, 'I have asked Rosa to show you to your room and bring you tea—English-style. I'm sure you would like the opportunity to freshen up after the journey and relax a little. I will see you later. We dine at nine-thirty.'

Quickly, she twisted round to look up at him, unashamed of the mute appeal in her eyes. But not quickly enough, because he was already strolling back towards the open main door, his hands in the side pockets of his beautifully cut, narrow-fitting trousers, completely relaxed. He had already forgotten she existed.

She wanted to cry out to him, to remind him that she was the woman he had married this morning, to beg him not to leave her alone like this. But she had her pride and did no such thing, and followed Rosa, her heels making lonely, echoing little sounds on the green Sardinian dressed-granite slabs beneath her feet.

Although the villa was single-storeyed, it was huge and rambling, with warren-like passages, different levels which meant trotting up a step or two and then, various yards and uncounted corners ahead, trotting down again. Confusing. By the time Rosa had opened one of the many arched doors with a flourish, Venetia knew she would never find her way back to the main hallway again. She should have remembered to bring a ball of string with her, she thought half hysterically, and quite forgot to smile as, within a welter of unintelligible conversation, Rosa retreated, bobbing and smiling.

Venetia sighed. She really would have to pull herself together. Rosa would think she was a boor. Never mind, she would probably grin from ear to ear in sheer relief at having been found again when the housekeeper appeared with that tea. Provided the other woman could remember where she was. The thought of staying mislaid forever brought a reluctant smile to her lips. That weird sense of unreality was impinging again, and it had nothing to do with the rambling villa and everything to do with the wall that had come between her and Carlo.

A wall she was going to have to dismantle, provided it wasn't merely a figment of her own imagination, she told herself tartly as she allowed her eyes to wander over the sumptuous room, lingering on the giant-sized bed.

And the more her eyes lingered, the more rapid her pulse-rate became, and her heart began to soar like a bird, because everything was going to be perfect for them. She had been a fool to imagine that anything had come between them, she assured herself as she discovered her suitcases on the far side of the bed and began, haphazardly, to unpack.

Carlo was only human; he had to be tired after the solid grind he had put in over the past few weeks. And besides, he was sophisticated, urbane, and had more than his fair share of Italian pride. He was not the type of man to leap on her and tear her clothes off at the very first opportunity!

The trouble was, she admitted wryly as she kicked off her shoes and curled her silk-covered toes into the rich deep-pile of the carpet, since meeting him again she had reverted to type—to the wildly passionate creature she had been at the age of eighteen!

One way or another, she was going to have to cultivate a little patience!

Venetia came awake slowly, drifting silkily to semi-consciousness, one hand curled beneath her cheek, her naked body cocooned beneath the soft duvet. Even though her eyes were still drowsily closed she knew the room was dark and, disorientated, she fumbled for the bedside lamp and finally managed to click it on.

Immediately, her eyes connected with the dress she had decided to wear for dinner tonight, hanging on one of the open wardrobe doors. It was a celebration of a dress, wickedly sexy in black silk moiré, a statement of her intention to turn her husband into her lover.

She slid the elegant length of her legs over the side of the bed and reached for the robe she had worn to drink the tea Rosa had brought up after she'd taken her bath, only now aware of what had woken her.

The sound of the shower in the connecting bathroom was suddenly cut off and the ensuing silence hung heavily. Carlo was back. He must have been gone for hours. Pushing her arms into the midnight-blue slither of silk, she tied the belt around her tiny waist, aware that her hands were actually shaking, her breath coming far too quickly, making her breasts push and peak against the thin fabric.

Cool it, she adjured herself swiftly. She had to try to be as adult and sophisticated about this as Carlo evidently was!

But she couldn't stop the crazy wings of excitement that fluttered around in her stomach like a million giant butterflies. And spiralling desire, as sweet and heavy as honey, made her clutch at the door-frame, her legs going useless as she walked into the bathroom and found him, a minute towel hitched around his waist, busily ridding himself of the day's growth of dark stubble in front of one of the many mirrors.

His body was superb and her throat went dry. He didn't turn, but she knew he had seen her through the mirror because his reflected eyes glittered darkly just for a moment before he said, 'Awake at last. You were tired and tense; I'm glad you were able to relax.'

So he had only been concerned for her well-being! She had been worried about something that didn't exist outside her head! Her heart singing, she padded swiftly to him, her bare feet making no sound on the granite floor-tiles.

'Where have you been?' Lovingly, she wrapped her arms around his nearly naked body, resting her head against the smooth, warm satin of his back, her fingertips caressing the hard, ridged muscles of his midriff, her body burning with the scorching flame of her desire for him. 'I missed you,' she murmured huskily, her mouth opening to taste the spiced honey of his skin. And she felt his body go taut and heard him say,

'Unlike you, *sposa mia*, this visit is not a complete holiday for me.' He twisted round, gently but firmly untwining her clinging arms, smiling crookedly down on her. 'I have vineyards here and I have spent the afternoon conferring with my manager.'

A weird way to spend a honeymoon! But Venetia could forgive him that, forgive him anything. And he had said it wouldn't be a complete holiday for him, so maybe the hours of work he had put in, while she had been taking the rest he had been caring enough to guess she needed, would leave the rest of his time here free to be with her.

She smiled at him mistily, all the love she had for him shining unashamedly in her eyes, and moved closer, her body needing to dissolve into his. But he set her aside, his hands firm, and touched a tiny lever that had one of the mirrored walls smoothly swinging aside to reveal an adjoining bedroom, a very masculine room, the ochres and browns and touches of russet contrasting markedly with the blues and creams of her room.

Her room! Separate rooms connected by this sumptuous bathroom.

She wouldn't let him see how much it hurt her. After all, she told herself staunchly, many couples preferred separate rooms—provided they were wealthy enough to afford the space.

She wasn't going to let him see her complete lack of sophistication here—no, of course she darn well wasn't! Or allow him to glimpse her insecurities. Of all the human beings she had met, he was the only one who had ever been able to make her feel insecure. And it was up to her to make sure that he spent far more time in her room than in his own!

'Love your room,' she said brightly, tipping her head on one side, her eyes wicked. 'Wouldn't you like to see mine?'

Her voice was husky with invitation and she could feel her breasts tingling, already peaking quite shamelessly against the fine silky fabric of her robe as his half-shuttered eyes made a slow, lazy assessment of her body. But all he said was, 'It holds no mysteries for me, I'm afraid. I have visited this villa for as long as I can remember. I am intimately familiar with every nook and cranny. Now, hurry and get dressed. We are already late and Rosa has gone to a great deal of trouble over dinner.'

Rats to Rosa! Venetia scowled at his retreating back then closed her eyes on the sting of tears. She was doing it again, she thought rigidly, looking for put-downs where there were none—except in her own over-active imagination.

Of course they were already late. She had slept much longer than she had meant to. And of course Rosa would have planned a lavish celebratory meal. Carlo didn't get married every day, did he? And of course Carlo wouldn't be thoughtless or discourteous enough to let all the housekeeper's preparations go to waste while he spent the evening in his wife's bed.

They had the rest of the night, the rest of their lives, she reminded herself as she marched back into her own room and began to get ready.

The wicked black dress fitted her like a second skin, the cleverly cut, tiny bodice secured by a narrow, crystal-encrusted halter strap, the short straight skirt revealing the endless silk-clad elegance of her legs. A more than usually dramatic choice of make-up completed the effect she had set out to achieve, and Carlo's magnificent eyes wouldn't be remote when he looked at her tonight!

She had spent a lot of time while he had been absent in the weeks before their marriage simply shopping for clothes that would please him. The sombre, understated garments she had chosen to suit her image during the barren years when they had been apart had all been bundled off to a charity shop with no regret whatsoever. In future she would dress to please her husband, to complement the passionate side of her nature that had been put into cold storage six years ago.

And the flash of fire in his black eyes told her all she needed to know before it was banked down, quenched by his formidable will as he escorted her down to dinner.

He was superb, she thought as she smiled intimately at him across the circular dining-table, flowers and candles making it festive. The sophisticated dinner-jacket he wore made him look suave, utterly dangerous, smoothing over yet undeniably enhancing the heart-stopping savagery of his male beauty.

Candlelight played like golden water over the formidably strong planes and angles of his face, making a mystery of what to her was so dear, so familiar, the beloved features as well known to her as her own, cherished—for so long, unknowingly—deep in the secret places of her heart.

Venetia's throat closed up with a happiness that was almost painful and she was able to do little more than push course after course of Rosa's splendidly, lovingly prepared meal around her plate. The exotic flavours of *bottarghe*, the creamy roe of the mullet and, according to Carlo, considered a great delicacy on the island, and *sa fregula*—a type of couscous—and succulent Sardinian artichokes were totally lost on her as she tried to concentrate on what Carlo was telling her about the island's chequered history.

But none of it sank in; she could only wish for the seemingly interminable meal to be over and done with, and when, after Luigi served the coffee and opened yet another bottle of wine, he and Rosa withdrew, she was almost incapable of movement, her relief was so great.

'You must try a little of this.' Carlo's eyes were sleepy as he rose lithely from the table, the newly opened wine bottle in his hand. 'Some of the best wines come from our vineyards around Alghero, but this is a Vernaccia from Oristano. Tell me if it is to your taste.'

'In a professional capacity?' Her smile was slow and sweet as she took the glass he handed her and got bonelessly to her feet. She lifted the glass and he answered her indifferently,

'As you like; be as professional as you please.' But there was no indifference in his eyes as they lingered on the tiny smile that curved the lush contours of her mouth, and her voice was husky as she denied,

'Not tonight,' and took a sip of the strong, sweet liquid, then held her glass to his lips, moving closer, her body a mere whisper away from the shattering male potency of his as she murmured, all unknowing seduction and bewitching eyes, 'A toast. To us, to our future.'

One of the candles fluttered and went out and the brief flare of its dying illuminated and heightened the autocratic severity of his features. Venetia shivered, and didn't know why, and shook her head slightly in unconscious repudiation, and quickly laid her hand palm downwards on the expensive black fabric that covered his broad chest.

Candlelight gleamed on the rich gold of the wide wedding-ring he had placed on her finger earlier today, and his voice was alive with hidden, unreadable nuances as he repeated, 'To our future,' and sipped from the glass she held to his lips. 'May it bring more pleasure than pain.'

'I won't argue with that!' She watched from sultry eyes as he set the glass aside, her long lashes lowered languorously, her blood running thickly, sweetly through her veins as she waited for him to take her in his arms, to claim all the loving she was so desperate to give. And she promised passionately, twining her arms around his neck, insinuating herself closer to the warm power of his body, 'Forget the pain; all I ever want to do is pleasure you, my love.'

Suddenly, he smiled, his lean, hard face looking down into hers, his black eyes burnished with hot intensity, with an emotion so strong that it seemed to feed upon her, sap her of all energy, so that, weakened, all she could do was cling to him, her boneless body melting into his, her fingers stroking the nape of his neck where the crisp dark hair sprang from the silk-covered steel of the base of his skull.

'Carlo...' His name was a whispered prayer on her lips as she eagerly sought his mouth, her whole body quivering in a passion of wild need as his hands shaped her breasts, her head spinning as he uttered an impatient growl and slid his hands roughly over the fragile span of her square shoulders to rip away the clasp that held the halter in place.

Abruptly, he tugged the black silk down towards her waist, exposing the twin globes of her pouting breasts, and his accent thickened sexily as his beautiful hands cupped her, murmuring, 'So much beauty. And so invitingly mine. All mine. To do with as I please?'

'Anything!' Venetia cried with hoarse abandon, her swollen nipples aching for the release of his moist, suckling mouth, and her hands reached beneath his jacket, fiercely clutching at the hard span of his ribcage as her legs threatened to buckle beneath her.

But he held her upright, dragging her hips into the heated span of his, holding her there so that the rising male power of him made her flesh ache in tumultuous, ecstatic anticipation.

He was a fever in her blood, a wildness that could never be tamed. He was her love, her mate, now and for always. She had recognised it six years ago and tonight that certainty was to be reinforced, bonding them so closely together that nothing could ever prise them apart.

And she breathed his name softly, with adoration, and closed her eyes in near delirium as he bent his dark head, the stark, hard contours of his features softening in the glow of candlelight as he took one peaked nipple into his mouth and laved it with his tongue.

And then the other, softly, wickedly teasing until her body was on fire for him, her breath coming in panting little moans that were partly agonised, unbelievable urgency, partly debilitating weakness, and wholly pleasure. And his hands found the tiny zip at the back of her dress, dealt with it, and helped the clinging fabric down over the curve of her hips.

It pooled at her feet in a whispering slither of silk, and he lifted her free and held her trembling body at arm's length. And she tilted her head back, candlelight gleaming on the dark, curving line of her hair as her smouldering eyes watched him watching her.

Clad now in only the merest triangle of black lace, her silk stockings naughtily suspended by the witchery of narrow scarlet garters, she was gloriously, unashamedly revelling in her near-nudity. She was his, had always been his. And now he was hers!

And dull patches of colour stained the chiselled angles of his cheekbones as his eyes lifted at last to lock with hers. And, just for a flicker of time, something savage and elemental exploded to life deep in the blackness of his gaze and, immediately, unstoppably, an answering pagan passion leapt to control her, and he saw it happen, she knew he did, because his face changed, went still, as if, inexplicably, he had been waiting for a moment such as this. Then his mouth curled contemptuously as he said in cool, killing tones, 'Enough, I think. Cover yourself.'

He turned with hatefully smooth insouciance, lifted his glass of Vernaccia, drained it and set it down slowly. And she stared at the etched disdain of his Roman profile, the brooding line of his mouth, the proud prominence of his chin, and her eyes were clouded with utter bewilderment because this simply could not be happening.

And yet it was.

She shivered convulsively, crossing her arms across her breasts, and her voice was stricken as she asked, 'Why?'

It was almost as if he had forgotten she was there, as if he had put her completely out of his mind, because the pinpoint of agony in her voice made him go rigid, the wide line of his shoulders straight and high. And then he did turn, but slowly, so slowly, and his face told her nothing of what was happening inside his head because there was nothing there. Only an impassive mask.

Briefly, his eyes held hers, the emptiness terrifying her until her whole world exploded in a passion of disbelief when he told her coolly, 'Revenge, *sposa mia*, revenge.' A glint of something diabolical formed in the dark enigma of his eyes. 'Revenge for the way you insulted my pride. Simply and unalterably that.'

CHAPTER TEN

THE cruelty of Carlo's words pierced Venetia like the blade of a knife and the sudden, awful pain of it drained the colour from her face.

Her brain was spiralling with a million questions, but her shock was too great to give them voice. Her mouth moved soundlessly and Carlo's hooded eyes swept slowly from her bloodless lips to the tips of her toes before he turned his back on her, telling her scathingly, 'Get dressed. Believe me, the sight of your nakedness will never tempt me to take you into my bed. I have finished with you.'

Humiliation made her feel physically ill. If she could have curled up and died right here on the spot then she would have willingly done so. And the dress she had worn—for him—wasn't the type one could simply slip on. Too shattered to do anything else, she clutched the discarded garment in front of her, like a shield, and lifted her stricken eyes to find that he had flung himself on to a heavily carved chair, leaning back, his long, beautifully made hands resting against the scrolled ends of the arm-rests.

'Why?' she forced through shock-numbed lips. 'Why revenge?'

He lifted wide shoulders in an eloquent shrug and leaned his head against the carved wooden back-rest, every line of his body a cold dismissal. And as her damaged senses struggled to assimilate the relaxed arrogance of his pose, anger began to riot hotly through her veins, and she drew a deep breath in through pinched nostrils.

How dared he demean her this way? Refuse to answer her? He looked for all the world like a medieval baron, above normal morality, normal human feelings. Contempt added a hateful patina to the cold austerity of his face, revealed most damningly in the brooding curve of his sensual mouth.

For a second, rage took her by the throat, shaking her. She wanted to claw that hateful mask with her nails, to rip it away and find the man she loved. But she controlled it, closing her eyes against the surging strength of the raging emotion, and when she eventually spoke it was with a cool contempt that measured up to his own.

'Cat got your tongue?'

He ignored the gibe, merely steepling his fingers, the tips resting against the wide curve of his lower lip, looking at her, and there was no way she could tell what he was thinking, because the opaque blackness of his eyes was shuttered by half-lowered olive-toned eyelids and the thick dark sweep of his lashes. And his voice was insultingly unemotive as he denied, 'Revenge is perhaps not the right word, although it does come into it. Looking after my financial interests in Ross UK was a part of my decision to marry you. Left alone, you could have given in to Carew's insistence that you sell up and get out and indulge your combined appetites on the proceeds. You were already talking of selling the family home, and, knowing of your continued sexual adventures together, I realised it wouldn't have taken much pressure from him to get you to agree to leave the company to go under. He already knew that his days of profit-milking were well and truly over. I couldn't allow that to happen, could I?' He closed his eyes, as if bored by the discussion. 'I don't think there's any more to be said on the subject.'

Walking out on him took all her courage. Dignity didn't come packaged in mere wisps of black silk and a pair of scarlet garters. But she couldn't listen to another word. Everything he said, every look he gave her, every action, tore at her heart until she was in danger of breaking up completely.

And that she would not do. Not in front of him.

Somehow she found her way back to her room and, thankfully, she had not been seen by Rosa or Luigi. That would have been the final shameful humiliation. And she couldn't wait to rid herself of that scandalous underwear, stuffing the sheer silk stockings, the frivolous briefs and the now pathetic scarlet garters into an empty suitcase to be disposed of as soon as she happened across a convenient bonfire or waste-bin.

All she wanted to do was cry herself to sleep, to find oblivion, shut out the pain of what had happened. But as she creamed off her make-up she knew it wouldn't be that easy. Today should have been the most wonderful day of her life, and Carlo had turned it into the blackest kind of comedy.

She hadn't known he could be so cruel.

How could he have pretended to want her and then, at the first practical opportunity after he had bound her to him by a wedding ceremony, demonstrate so evilly that he didn't want her at any price?

He had spoken, enigmatically, of revenge. It was a cold, disgusting little word and it made her shiver. And she knew, feeling not too pleased about it, that, come what may, she had to hear him tell her exactly why he imagined he had the right to take it.

Before she left him, sought an annulment, she had to learn the truth. Or what passed for the truth in that twisted, diabolical mind of his!

Acting on impulse, before her courage deserted her, she yanked the tie-belt of her robe more tightly around her tiny waist and stamped through the bathroom, into his room.

He wasn't there. Had she really expected him to be? she wondered raggedly. But she could wait. She could wait all night, for the rest of her life, if need be. Because, until she knew his reasons, was shown a glimpse of the black depths of his soul, she would know no peace, no rest.

And, when she knew, she would waste no more emotion on him, would cut him out of her heart and out of her life. He had killed all her love, all her hopes, with a slashing cruelty that still left her breathless, and he was going to have to explain why. He owed her that much.

Dawn was breaking when he finally walked into the room. Venetia's eyes were gritty from lack of sleep, her nerves stretched to a screaming-point so that she almost yelled, Where the hell do you think you've been? But she swallowed the scalding words because to utter them would have made her sound like a suspicious wife.

And she wasn't a wife, was she? And she saw his eyes harden in his haggard face as she faced him from the heaped pillows on his bed where she had taken weary refuge a couple of hours ago.

'I'm sorry you had a wasted night,' he said with toneless sarcasm. 'I thought I'd made it clear that I didn't want you in my bed. Ever.'

'So you did.' She affected a tiny yawn, tapping her teeth with the tips of her fingers. If he could play games then so could she. He looked as if he'd spent the night in hell, his black tie gone, his shirt undone at the collar, his face grey with something more than fatigue. And for some unfathomable reason his air of exhaustion, the world-weary look in his black, black eyes gave her a feeling of exultation that was hard to explain away.

She didn't try.

She was beginning to hate him.

'I'm perfectly capable of cutting my losses.' The look she gave him as she slid bonelessly to her feet was pure coquetry, purposely so. He had humiliated her utterly, but wasn't going to be allowed to know he had. So she looked into the hard, ravaged face and smiled. And told him carelessly, 'You win some, you lose some. You're not the only pebble on my beach, my dear Carlo. But before I pack my bags, I'd like to know precisely why you believe you have the right to take revenge. You owe me that much after making me endure that farce of a wedding ceremony.'

Throwing herself recklessly into the part she was playing, she gave him a mocking smile and shuddered, suddenly pushed back to stark, cold reality as something terrifying looked out of those hard black eyes.

And he said, not troubling to hide the bitterness, 'You don't change, do you? Once a slut, always a slut.'

Venetia went cold with rage. The short-lived pretence was over. She was through with playing games. Lifting her hand, she cracked it against his face, felt the sting of the impact in her fingers, the harsh abrasion as her soft skin met his dark overnight stubble. And heard him curse, his own hand snaking out to clamp around her wrist, forcing her to her knees in brutal retaliation. Then he flung her arm away as if the touch of her flesh disgusted him, untamed violence flaring in his eyes.

Venetia dropped her head, shivering with reaction as she knelt on the floor, the blue silk of her robe pooling around her. And heard him say, ice-cold and perfectly in control again, 'The ceremony we took part in was no farce, and you know it. You are my legal wife and so you will remain. Let there be no talk of bag-packing, until I am ready to tell you to do so, and no thoughts of seeking your freedom through divorce unless you want to see the business your father, and his father before him, built up to what it is today, sold off like so much dead wood, with the loss of a great many jobs. I do hope I make myself clear?'

Perfectly, horribly, hopelessly clear.

He was moving around the room now. From the rustle of his clothing she knew he was stripping. But it didn't matter. Nothing mattered. Tears formed achingly at the back of her eyes, but she'd be damned if she'd break down and cry in front of him. She sniffed, and he said conversationally, 'That being settled, I will ask you a question. In answering it truthfully you will find the reason behind my desire to punish you.'

She shrugged. Even that small movement was an effort. She didn't like riddles and did his reasons really matter any more? Did anything matter?

Reluctantly, she forced herself to look up at him. His feet were bare and he had stripped to the waist, and her mouth went dry just looking at him, at the olive-toned skin lightly roughened with crisp black hair, the rangy breadth of his shoulders, the sleek muscles of the deep chest that tapered down to a narrow, firm waist and almost non-existent hips. Need and wanting leapt to instant, insistent life inside her and she couldn't breathe for the sheer, bludgeoning power of it.

Hating her reaction, totally ashamed of it, she dropped her eyes and bit out harshly, 'Well? What do you want to know?' In a minute she would get up off her knees and beat a dignified retreat to her own room. When she felt stronger. When her legs began to feel more like flesh and bone and less like water.

'When you were eighteen years old, did you practically beg me to make love to you, tell me you loved me?'

It was the very last question she had expected him to ask, and everything went very still. She had to listen hard to discover if she was still breathing. And into the waiting silence she could sense his watchfulness and knew that if there was a purpose behind his question it wouldn't be pleasant.

But nothing he could do or say could make her hurt any more than she was already hurting. Nothing could be more painful than what had happened during this long and terrible night. So she replied dully, beyond caring, 'You know I did.' She got then to her feet, still shaky, no nearer understanding him than before. But there was a limit to what she could take right now. She had to be alone. She had to think.

But he moved in front of her, blocking her way. She shuddered. He was so close and yet, irrevocably, so distant. Instinctively, she ached to touch him, to trail her fingers over the sleek muscles of his lean male magnificence, but she closed her eyes to block out the sight of his near-nakedness, fiercely quelling the almost overwhelming temptation.

She had to be strong; she had to learn to hate and despise him. She had to! To allow him to suspect that, even now, she wanted him with every last fibre of her being would be to lay herself open to his cruel brand of humiliation. And then she heard the sudden, rough intake of his breath, the only sign of emotion he had shown all day, heard the bitterness in his dark voice as he said, 'You had the morals of an alley cat even then. One man, provided he was reasonably presentable, was virile and willing, was as good as another. However——' he gave a small shrug '—although I never forgot that time, I did forgive. You were barely eighteen years old and, to give you the benefit of the doubt, you probably didn't know what you were doing——'

Venetia had had enough. Once she had loved him and now she hated him! And she spat at him, her voice strangled with the birth pains of loathing, 'You insult me!'

'Do I? I wonder?'

She had made to sweep past him, but he kept her where she was by the baleful glare of his eyes, the sardonic, taunting curl of his mouth, and his voice dropped to a hateful whisper as he repeated, 'I wonder, *sposa mia*. If I touch you...here, and here...' Lean, olive-toned fingers caressed each nipple in turn, burning through the blue silk, and Venetia shuddered with helpless shame as each bud tautened into immediate, inviting life. 'So you see how you respond instinctively, even to a man who has humiliated and degraded you?' Both hands were now fondling the hardened mounds of her breasts, caressing, stroking, holding, and white-hot heat raged deep inside her and she moaned rawly in fierce self-condemnation, the softness of his voice burning into her brain. 'Any man will do, my insatiable little wanton. I, however, have no intention of playing stud to any woman, no matter how desirable.'

Fuelled by the energy of despair and self-disgust, Venetia thrust his hands away, her breath sobbing in her chest as his tone hardened abrasively. 'I had no idea what you were when you tormented me with your passion and beauty all those years ago. I even believed you when you spoke of love. I even believed myself in love with you! And you tempted me with what you offered—oh, how you tempted me!' Bitterness made his voice savage and she flicked him a look from empty, uncomprehending eyes, trying to look into the past, but failing, because the present was killing her, tearing her to tiny pieces.

And his eyes were unforgiving, the taunting line of his mouth was for his own folly as he told her, 'But I did the honourable thing. I spoke to your father, told him how I burned to possess you, bind you to me. He was pleased, I know. He couldn't have known what you were. He agreed with my suggestion that you and I become betrothed—for a trial period of at least a year. I was mature enough to trust my feelings, but, at eighteen, I felt you were too young to be able to trust your own. *Santa Maria*!' His voice was a knife-cut of self-derision. 'I was a fool! I came to you, hurried to find you, to tell you what I had decided. And found you, almost naked, enjoying sex with Carew!' His voice was deadly now, cold and low. 'However, as I have already explained, after I had recovered from the damage to my pride, I forgave. But when I returned, out of respect for your father, I found you still together. Did you have an unwritten contract to satisfy each other's urges when required, no strings? Even continuing the sordid relationship after his marriage? No matter...' he dismissed with a decisive slash of one hand. 'The future is all that matters. Your future as my wife. The wanton will be chaste. I have no intention of satisfying your animal urges, and don't even think of taking a lover. I would kill him with as little compunction as I would step on an ant! That, *sposa mia*, is your punishment for trying to make a fool of me. That, my dear, is my revenge.'

Venetia looked helplessly into his eyes, unable to control the shudders that raked through her slender body. His eyes were glittering with naked contempt in his stony face and she uttered thickly, trying to make him see how wrongly he had judged her, 'It was nothing like that——'

But he cut her short with a violent obscenity, his mouth curling with contempt as he grated, 'Spare me your sick lies! I might almost have believed you changed had I not walked into a room and seen you in your lover's arms, heard him trying to persuade you against marriage to me. Had I not returned earlier than you had expected I would not have known about that sordid assignation. Had you invited him round to assure him that, even though you would be married to me, nothing would change? To explain that marriage to me would give you the financial security you needed while leaving you free to satisfy your prodigious sexual appetites whenever my back was turned? I would have married you in good faith, hoping for a future with you, but when I saw the two of you together all that changed,' he told her grimly. 'The marriage had to take place, of course. The announcement had been made and the arrangements were in hand. But, more importantly, it suited my business plans, the desire I had to bring the two companies back together. And, not least, I saw the opportunity to punish you, make you pay for being the wanton you are. No one tries to trick me, use me, and gets away with it.' He swore again, but coldly, stepping back. 'Go. I have had enough. Go to your room and begin to reconcile yourself to having to endure a nun-like existence for the rest of your tainted life!'

CHAPTER ELEVEN

VENETIA didn't know how far she had walked, where she was, or whether she would ever find her way back to the villa again. She didn't care, either.

She trudged on, the sun beating down from a cloudless blue sky. Eagles soared overhead and wild sheep grazed the short, flower-spiked, herb-grown grass, but she was oblivious. She couldn't, wouldn't go on as she was.

During the two days she had been in Sardinia she had seen Carlo only once—apart from that traumatic first night—and that had been at dinner last evening. It was the only attempt he had made at keeping up appearances, talking to her, with a bland politeness that had made her want to scream, about what he had been doing that day, where he had been, telling her urbanely that she had no need to feel herself a prisoner, that Luigi would drive her anywhere she wanted to go. He understood little English and spoke even less, but he was intelligent enough to understand if she expressed a desire to go somewhere in particular.

She hadn't listened, hadn't made any replies, had eaten little and drunk more wine than was wise, not caring what Rosa and Luigi might think of such a sullen bride, a bridegroom who had absented himself all day. Not caring about anything, because what was the point?

Carlo wouldn't listen to anything she might say in her own defence. His opinion of her was entrenched and wouldn't go away. And although he had at times shown, demonstrably, that he desired her body, he had too much pride, too much will-power to allow himself to be ensnared by physical needs.

And she no longer wanted to ensnare him, anyway. She hated him. And she was going to fight for her own survival, forget she had ever loved him more than life itself. She was not going to be trapped here, a forsaken wife in a foreign land. She was going to have to do something about her unenviable, untenable situation. But carefully. She couldn't put all those jobs back home at risk.

And last night, after Rosa and Luigi had withdrawn, leaving her facing him across the dinner-table, she had risen to her feet, dropping her linen napkin in the mangled remains of her virtually untouched meal, and told him unemotionally, 'It's a pity that your pride has blinded you to the truth. You married a virgin.'

His black brows had drawn together in a thunderous frown and she had smiled then, thinly, turning her back on him as she had walked from the room, tossing brittly over her shoulder, 'And now you'll never find out if I'm telling the truth, will you? Enjoy your revenge; I hope it keeps you warm at night!'

And that, she had vowed, was the very last time she would ever speak to him.

She sighed, rubbing the tips of her fingers over her hot forehead. She had given herself today to come up with a solution to her problems. And she thought she had found it. Dropping down over the brow of a stone-crowned hill, she saw the villa in front of her, half a mile or so distant, and took it as an omen. She had come back full circle at the precise moment when her vague plans for getting away had coalesced into a viable whole.

Rosa met her as she hurried in through the main door, her mind too preoccupied with what she had to do to even notice, and be grateful for, the welcome coolness. It was almost midday. If yesterday was to set the pattern, then Carlo wouldn't put in an appearance until it was time to change for dinner. He would be spending his day with his employees at the vineyards, his friends, as far away from her as he could get.

'Lunch,' Rosa said hopefully, then babbled away in her own language, but Venetia shook her head, managing, by way of mime, to indicate her need for a telephone. The penny dropping, Rosa beamed with self-congratulation and led the way, with many gesticulations, to a huge study, hovering while Venetia worked her way through the directory until she found the number she wanted.

She knew, because during the weeks before her wedding she had read every travel book featuring Sardinia that she could lay her hands on, that there were frequent internal flights between Alghero and Cagliari, so that was no worry. But she needed a connection to London, and she got it. Luck was with her, she thought, but, strangely, found little comfort in it.

There was enough time. The flight to London didn't leave until the evening. But she didn't want to linger. She couldn't wait to get away and gave heartfelt thanks for having had the foresight to bring her credit card with her.

She changed quickly into lightweight stone-coloured trousers topped by a sleeveless black silk blouse, stuffed a few necessary toiletries into her leather shoulder-bag, and draped a black and cream striped linen blazer over her arm, not bothering to take back any of the clothes she'd brought with her for the honeymoon that hadn't taken place, because she didn't want to be reminded of how deliriously happy she'd been when she'd bought them.

The letter to Carlo had been the first thing she'd attended to, and she hoped it said enough to stop him rushing out and wreaking havoc on the family business back in England. In it she had stated her promise not to file for divorce, to remain, nominally, his wife. She would continue to work at the headquarters of Ross UK, under his direction, and would be available to see him whenever he thought it necessary for them to meet.

She left it, sealed in an envelope, on his bed.

'Alghero,' she said to Luigi, when she ran him to earth polishing the limo in one of the garages. 'The airport.'

'*Signora*?' He looked totally perplexed and Venetia frowned, using one hand to imitate a plane taking off, and Luigi nodded. 'Airport, I understand.' But he was still looking puzzled as he rolled down the sleeves of his white shirt and reached his lightweight jacket from a hook on the back of one of the doors. And the drive was completed in silence, Venetia heartily thankful that neither could converse in the other's language.

But he hovered, like an anxious guardian angel, while she purchased her ticket for the three thirty-five flight to Cagliari, and stood watching as she crossed the tarmac shimmering in the warmth of the spring sunlight, the other passengers forming a shield between her and his obvious discomfort.

One of the male passengers just ahead of her was, superficially, so like Carlo that her heart missed a beat then twisted agonisingly inside her. If just the set of a pair of wide, masculine shoulders, the back of an arrogantly held dark head could have her consumed with unlooked for, unwanted emotional longings, then what hope was there for her?

Tears blinded her and she stumbled. She couldn't just go like this, simply walk away. One way or another, she was going to have to try to make him understand that she wasn't what he thought she was.

Righting herself, retrieving the blazer that had fallen from her arm, she felt a supportive hand beneath her elbow, heard someone saying something in Italian, looked up and caught the concern in the stewardess's eyes.

'I'm sorry,' she muttered, rubbing at the tears that were unaccountably streaming down her face, repeating stupidly, 'I'm sorry.'

'Ah—English.' The dark-eyed girl gave a sympathetic smile. 'You are unwell? Can I help?'

Everyone else had boarded now. Venetia knew she shouldn't be here. She wasn't a coward, not normally. She had to find Carlo. Convince him. She shook her head, stepping backwards, her voice thick and unsteady as she said, 'I'm sorry. I can't take this flight. I've just realised . . .' She turned and walked quickly back into the shade of the terminal building. Luckily Luigi hadn't waited to see the plane take off, and there was no sign of the car outside. The last thing she wanted was to be escorted straight back to the villa just now. She needed time to think clearly, to recover from the emotional attack that had made her act like a first-class fool out there on the tarmac.

Hiring a taxi to take her to Alghero was no problem. Fortunately she had brought her own supply of lire with her, intending to buy souvenirs for her friends back home, not expecting Carlo to do it for her, because she valued her independence.

The driver dropped her off in the centre of the popular resort and in normal circumstances she would have been excited at the prospect of exploring the beautiful city with its mixture of ancient and modern buildings, the old town with its fortifications, narrow streets and imposing towers. But these were far from normal circumstances and Venetia wandered, without really knowing where she was going, down towards the harbour.

Finding a small pavement café, she sat in the shade of a striped umbrella and ordered a fruit juice which she forgot to drink.

She felt calmer now, but it was the calmness of the acceptance of defeat, she recognised, accepting the dull, permanent ache beneath her breastbone along with everything else.

Her justifiable rage at what Carlo had done had gone now and all that was left behind was a dreadful, aching sadness. There had been a chance for them, once. She could still hear Carlo telling her that he had believed he loved her six years ago, had been prepared to wait for her. Once, he had wanted to marry her for love. Once, a long time ago. Then six years later he had proposed. He had wanted control of the business, true, but he had also wanted her. And one day, she was sure, he would have grown to love her, especially if she had been able to make him believe that her past was not what he had thought it to be. And, again, Simon had ruined everything for her.

She shifted restlessly in her seat, her blank eyes not registering anything of the colourful scene, looking backwards as she mourned for what might have been.

Carlo had even spoken to her father, formally asking the older man's permission for a betrothal. She hadn't fully taken it all in before now. When he had spat out the details of what had happened on that fateful day in that long-gone summer, she had been too shell-shocked by what had gone before to register the sad facts of what he had been actually telling her: that once he had loved her.

And now she saw the threads of Simon's grasping duplicity quite clearly. When she had been eighteen he had hardly been able to keep his hands off her. Not because he had truly felt anything for her, but because he'd been entrusted with escort duty and had seen his opportunity. Marrying the boss's daughter would have suited him down to the ground. And during the following years he had bided his time, regaining her trust, putting himself out to help her when she'd joined the company—and all the while taking dishonest hand-outs. Even when Angie had tricked him into marriage he hadn't entirely given up. One of the first things he'd done after Carlo had fired him had been to come to her with those preposterous suggestions!

But she couldn't even rake up enough anger to want to throttle the devious, crooked swine! Her emotions were spent, only sad hopelessness left to keep her company. That, and the forlorn hope that Carlo might, just somehow, be persuaded to listen to her side of the story.

Someone at one of the adjoining tables had a transistor radio blaring out pop music, and Venetia only noticed the noise pollution when it stopped. And then the brief but blessed silence was filled by the voice of an Italian announcer giving a news flash—bad news, too, Venetia registered, not understanding a word but observing the shocked reactions of the local patrons around her.

Pulling a sigh, Venetia forgot the small commotion going on around her as unintelligible voices were raised in a babble of conjecture—or was it outrage?—at the end of the announcement, her thoughts homing in immediately on the problem that faced her.

Carlo felt nothing but contempt for her now, she knew that and, in a strange, fatalistic way, accepted it. Accepted the bitterness, the damaged Italian male pride that had made him do what he had. But if she could make him listen and, what was more important, believe her side of the story, then they could part with far less enmity on his side. Eventually, they might even become friends, as well as business partners.

Her mangled heart came back to consciousness, twisting and bucking painfully inside her. Friendship wasn't what she wanted. She wanted him! But she couldn't have him, she reminded herself crossly, blinking back the tears that she had mistakenly believed all spent. All she could hope for was to achieve a kind of peace between them.

She was stiff with sitting, she realised, noticing one of the waiters giving her a sidelong, slightly suspicious glance. She had no idea how long she'd been here, but the sun was low in the sky, and if she wanted to find a taxi to get her back to the villa before Carlo returned then she ought to make a move.

Taking a sip of her now tepid fruit juice, she collected her things and got stiffly to her feet, leaving a handsome tip to justify the length of time she had occupied this table. She was going to have to get Carlo to listen to her, and hope he could put his bitterness aside and begin to believe her.

Trouble was, she acknowledged miserably as she walked to the edge of the pavement, looking for a cruising taxi, she had probably spiked her own guns. The reckless things she'd said to him, merely in retaliation for the verbal blows he had dealt her, would have reinforced his already rock-bottom opinion of her. That alone was going to make her task a thousand times more difficult!

Hopeless. And should she really even try? Perhaps she should stick to her original decision and get to Cagliari? She would be far too late to get the evening flight to London but, using her international credit card, she could book into a hotel and wait for the first available flight back home. Why put herself through the further misery of trying to convince the unconvincible?

Indecision had her rooted to the spot, oblivious of the rush of traffic, until the screech of brakes and the slam of a car door almost under her nose had her stepping back, knocking against one of the café tables.

'*Cristo*!'

Crowded back by a hard male body, gripped by manacles of steel, Venetia's breath was knocked out of her lungs as Carlo lunged at her, the car he had been driving slewed across the road. He must have returned earlier than he had done yesterday, discovered her defection, and come to drag her back. Back to the villa to wreak his vengeance. Panic made her heartbeat accelerate until she felt it would burst out of her chest, and she tried to beat him off, her small fists flailing impotently against his immovable body.

'Venetia, thank God. Oh, thank God!' Strong, inescapable arms dragged her against the length of his body, his face buried in her hair, his lips murmuring endearments in his own language, his voice ragged with raw passion. 'Is it really you? Please, God, I'm not dreaming!'

She was trembling in his arms, unable to understand. He was holding her as if he would never let her go, his need for punitive vengeance forgotten, or so it seemed. Then, reluctantly, he released her, but only by enough to search her face with hungry, ravaged, red-rimmed eyes.

Still shaken, Venetia gazed up at him perplexedly, hardly able to believe that this was happening at all, completely shattered when she saw the unmistakable glitter of moisture in his black, black eyes. And her own throat clogged with tears when he said rawly, 'I thought you were dead. Dead, or at the very least seriously maimed. I could have killed myself for grief!'

There was no mistaking the intensity of his emotion and, although she couldn't understand his violent change of attitude, an answering passion filled her veins with fire and her breath clogged in her throat, her voice barely audible as she said thickly, 'Carlo—I don't understand. Why did you think I was dead?' It didn't make any kind of sense, none at all, until he answered her quickly, still sounding shaken,

'I spent the morning on the estate, working, trying to stop myself from thinking. The punishment I'd planned was hurting me far more than it was hurting you and I suddenly knew I had to make an end of it.' The hands that were gripping hers tightened until she thought every slender bone would break beneath the pressure, but didn't care. He could break every bone in her body and she would still love him! And he was telling her, his voice raw, 'I suddenly realised what I had been too blind to see—that I wanted you as I have never wanted any other woman. That by refusing to consummate our marriage I was denying myself far more than I was denying you. That I didn't care how many lovers you had had in the past—only that there would be no more in the future. Except me, of course! I went straight back to the villa, determined to ask your forgiveness, to begin our married life.'

There was a decidedly proprietorial glint in the black eyes now and the colour was beginning to come back into his ashen face. Venetia went a little cold. She had always known, even six years ago, that he wanted her body. And if he had decided to ask her to forgive him the unforgivable, and take her to his bed, then that was a step in the right direction. Or was it? Was she being greedy, wanting so very much more?

'Don't look like that,' he commanded roughly, pulling her head into the angle of her shoulder. 'I demand that you allow me some hope.'

He sounded so typically arrogant that she couldn't prevent the tiny smile that curved her lush mouth. As ever, he demanded...

'There's more,' he ground out thickly, and she felt a huge shudder rake through his magnificent body. 'When I got back to the villa I asked where you were. Luigi told me you'd gone to the airport, that he'd taken you himself and seen you board the three thirty-five shuttle for Cagliari. He believed I must have known. I was still in control, even after I read your letter. I phoned the airport and asked them to give the Rossi jet clearance for take-off, and phoned the company pilot and told him to get ready, at once. I reckoned I still had time to prevent you boarding the flight for London which, I guessed, was what you had in mind. It was then I was told that the plane you'd been on had crashed on landing, killing or seriously maiming crew and passengers. It was then——' he dragged in a deep, shuddering breath '—that I knew I loved you more than life itself. That I'd lost you, without ever having been able to tell you that simple truth. I wanted to die.'

'Oh, Carlo!' She turned her head, lifting it to plant hungry, yet tender kisses down the corded length of his throat. He loved her, that was the only thing that mattered. Then she shuddered violently, the impact of what he had told her only now sinking in. If it hadn't been for one of the male passengers bearing a superficial likeness to Carlo, she would have been on that plane. She gave a short prayer of anguished sympathy for all those who had suffered and then asked shakily, between kisses, 'Then what were you doing here, looking for me?' Not that it really mattered, of course. Knowing how he had suffered, believing her to have been on that ill-fated plane, knowing that in that moment of trauma he had recognised how much he loved her, was the only thing that mattered at all, she thought, tilting her head back, the better to nibble the lobe of his ear.

'I wasn't looking for you,' he denied huskily, his hands beginning to caress her back, sliding down to her neat bottom, pressing her closer and ever closer. 'I was driving to the airport—like a maniac, I must admit. The only hope I could cling on to was that you were still alive. And no matter how injured, I would move heaven and earth to make you well again, beg you to give me the chance to make you love me, to forgive me. And then I saw you. Just standing there. *Cristo*! I thought you were a ghost—I couldn't believe you were flesh and blood, a warm and living woman, until I took you in my arms and held you!' His sensual mouth hovered above her own, and she couldn't believe that her proud Carlo was actually pleading with her until he begged, 'Promise me you will give me the opportunity to make reparation, give me the chance to make you love me all over again? I think you did, once, just a little. Will you try? Please?'

Her Carlo—humble? A smile lit her pale, slanting eyes as she looked deep into his, gratified to find all that daunting pride winging straight back as she told him simply, 'No problem. I tried to stop loving you, but couldn't. I'll love you until I die.'

And then he kissed her. And it was glorious, like being transported to heaven on the back of a rainbow, the world disintegrating around them both in a million glittering shards of fabulously coloured lights, and Venetia's soul only came down to ground level again when clinging lips parted for want of breath and the cacophony around them impinged on her consciousness.

She went scarlet. Ever since Carlo had leapt out of that car, the crowd had obviously been gathering. And now the huge mass of onlookers were stamping their feet, clapping hands, whistling and cheering. And, just for the heck of it, car horns were hooting in crazy competition, drivers stopping to see what was going on, adding to the traffic jam already caused by Carlo's limo blocking most of the narrow street.

But there wasn't a bone of embarrassment in Carlo's magnificent body, she recognised with grudging admiration, her own embarrassment beginning to recede as, with typical Italian macho pride, he bowed to the crowd in all directions, his white smile that of an acknowledged conquering hero, his head arrogantly high as he took her hand and tucked it in the crook of his arm, escorting her through the cheerful crowd which fell back in front of them like the Red Sea.

And he was still grinning widely after the traffic jam had been miraculously sorted out and they headed home towards the villa. But then he said, only a little more seriously, 'It is fate. It has all been fate, ever since I saw you walk into a room, walk over to me with that provocative wiggle, and kiss me. I think, from that moment, I was a lost man. Oh——' he gave her a dazzling smile before turning his attention back to the road '—I tried to fight it. Kept telling myself to keep you at arm's length. You were too young for me. Too young to know your own mind, let alone have any inkling of what you were doing to me. *Santa Maria*—what you did to me! And then——' his voice went suddenly dark '—after I had mentally given in to the inevitable and spoken to your father, I found you with Simon. My humiliation and bitterness was intense—as I'm sure you have realised by now!'

Venetia could have cried. If only she hadn't forbidden her father to mention his name in her presence, she would have learned about that conversation, about the proposed betrothal! And could have done something to put matters right—written to Carlo, perhaps, explaining everything, before it had become too late, before the iron had entered his soul! They had been separated for years, unnecessarily, because she had refused to have his name mentioned!

No wonder her father had been stupefied by her refusal to listen to anything concerning Carlo Rossi. He had probably supposed that Carlo had mentioned his intentions to her, naturally enough. And that she had refused him, point-blank. Being a sensitive soul, he would have kept his own counsel, deciding it best not to bring the matter up in his subsequent phone conversations with the man who had declared his interest in becoming his son-in-law!

And now was the time to put matters right.

'Carlo,' she began staunchly. 'About Simon——'

'To hell with Simon!' he said rudely. 'He's in the past.' Then, far more calmly, 'I didn't come back to England with revenge in mind—I want you to understand that, *cara*. I came to your father's funeral primarily because I respected him a great deal. And I needed to look at ways and means to put the UK company on a sounder financial footing. Also, your father had died leaving the unfinished business with Carew. I was actually surprised by the extent of my bitterness when I saw you and Carew together. It was then, I think, that I realised how you had spoilt me for other women and the idea of marrying you to bring the company under the Rossi umbrella took root in my mind. I was willing to give it a go—how willing I didn't fully understand until I did some soul-searching this morning. I cut short my trip back home because I was missing you, only to find you'd made an assignation with Carew—why else would he have turned up like that, with you ready and waiting for him in that slinky thing you were wearing?'

There was a growl of temper in his voice and Venetia thought hollowly, Here we go again! and wondered if she should have one last try to make him listen to the truth. But he wasn't in a listening mood, wanting to get all his perceived sins finally off his chest.

'When I walked in and saw you in his arms, heard the crazy things he was saying, my first impulse was to wash my hands of you, as I had done before. But that soon disappeared beneath the sudden realisation of exactly how I could revenge myself on the woman I still didn't properly realise had been in my blood for years!' He expelled a huge sigh, as if relieved to have got it off his chest, out of the way, and, as the villa came into sight, he put his hand briefly on her thigh.

'And now I refuse to talk of the past again. Or even think of it. Our future is all that matters. As far as we are concerned, our lives together begin now. And I fully intend to make sure that you will never even want to look at another man again. I will be as much as you can handle!' he stated, all the male confidence in the world in the tone of his voice, the arrogant tilt of his head.

'Why didn't you tell me?' Carlo demanded, propping himself up on one elbow, the bedside lamp making his skin look like oiled silk, emphasising the deep frown-line between his brooding eyes.

'You wouldn't let me,' Venetia stated, a thread of mischief running through her husky voice. Making love with Carlo had been everything she'd ever dreamed it would be. And more. So much more. Her body was still throbbing with the wonderful aftermath, desire tightening inside her again as she remembered each glorious, loving moment.

Striding into the villa, Carlo had scooped her up into his arms and carried her to his bedroom, right under Rosa's and Luigi's fascinated eyes, only pausing to ask Luigi to put a bottle of champagne on ice and bring it through. Luigi had jumped to attention, she recalled, grinning all over his weathered face, doubtless giving up the attempt to make any sense of the bride and groom's erratic behaviour!

They had made undressing each other into an art form, and pleasuring each other something else again. And the only slight hiccup during the long, sensual hours of extremely erotic lovemaking had come when he had discovered her virgin state.

But by then, of course, it had been too late for questions. And now, on the languorous descent from heaven, Carlo rubbed a thumb over her lower lip and said wonderingly, 'You didn't play with married men. Simon was never your lover. No man was.' A frown of reproach darkened his brow. 'Why did you lead me to believe you were almost entirely without morals?'

'I think I must have been crazy,' she confessed, closing her eyes with sensual delight as his fingers stroked the length of her throat. 'The last time I'd seen you, you'd looked at me as if I were a tramp, beneath contempt. And when I saw you again I knew that nothing had changed. I still reacted to you as if you were the only man on earth——' she turned her head to put a kiss on the pulse-beat at the base of his throat '—and you still looked at me with contempt. I guess I said those things in self-defence. Stupid, wasn't it?'

'We were both stupid. Love made fools of us,' he affirmed. 'But, for love of you, I decided at last to forget all your past misdemeanours, make a fresh start, ensure that you wanted only me in future. Until today I hadn't really come to terms with the fact that for six years you'd been in my blood, spoiling me for any other woman. And even when I found you with Carew, that second time, and vowed I'd marry you simply to punish you, I wasn't telling myself the whole truth.' He gave a shuddering sigh, confessing, 'The truth is that I had to possess you, own you, in any circumstances. I have never before thought of myself as a stupid man, but even when, on the night I'd asked you to marry me, I went to your room to beg you to talk to me—to put my proposal in gentler terms—and found you missing, and went nearly crazy with anxiety, I still didn't realise how much I loved you. I thought it was merely lust, a need that wouldn't go away. It took an air crash to make me realise that I love you more than life.' He shuddered, his eyes turning momentarily bleak, before saying teasingly, 'But there is one thing that puzzles me.' Again his thumb stroked her kiss-bruised lips. 'I know now that I was the first for you—but what the hell was happening when I walked in on you and that creep? Twice!'

And so she told him, leaving nothing out, adding, 'After he'd jumped me as I got out of the pool I scarcely set eyes on him for a couple of years. I stopped socialising, started working, tried to change myself, tried to stop loving you. And he must have been desperate that last time. He'd lost his job—deservedly—probably realised he'd never get a reference. His marriage was in ruins and—well, I guess he thought he'd chance his arm. He tried to make me believe he'd loved me all along and couldn't wait to rub in the fact that you were merely marrying me for business reasons.'

She smiled up at him mistily, knowing that at last he understood, explaining, 'He'd been a great help to me when I'd been learning the business, and he couldn't have been more supportive after Father died. I had begun to look on him as a friend, but nothing more. I never did fancy him, not even remotely.'

'And why didn't you explain all this?' Carlo asked, tilting his head on one side, his eyes soft and loving, and Venetia reminded pertly,

'I tried to. Remember? At about the sixth attempt I just gave up and decided to let you find out for yourself.' She nipped the soft pad of his thumb, but gently, lovingly, and he said, his voice thickening,

'Witch! Mastering you will not be a push-over!'

'But no doubt you'll try?'

Venetia wriggled her hips, snuggling closer to him. And his voice wasn't the only thing that had thickened, she thought deliriously, wriggling again, and he told her huskily, his accent suddenly very pronounced, 'Always.

Again and again. I never give up.' And the last words she heard, before they rode the senses to heaven again, were the adoring affirmations of his love as he whispered, '*Bellissima* ... *Bellissima* ...!'

Next Month's Romances

Each month you can choose from a wide variety of romance with Mills & Boon. Below are the new titles to look out for next month, why not ask either Mills & Boon Reader Service or your Newsagent to reserve you a copy of the titles you want to buy – just tick the titles you would like and either post to Reader Service or take it to any Newsagent and ask them to order your books.

Please save me the following titles:	Please tick	√
TO TAME A WILD HEART	Emma Darcy	
ISLAND ENCHANTMENT	Robyn Donald	
A VALENTINE FOR DAISY	Betty Neels	
PRACTISE TO DECEIVE	Sally Wentworth	
FLAME ON THE HORIZON	Daphne Clair	
ROMAN SPRING	Sandra Marton	
LOVE OR NOTHING	Natalie Fox	
CLOSE CAPTIVITY	Elizabeth Power	
TOTAL POSSESSION	Kathryn Ross	
LOST LADY	Lee Wilkinson	
GIFT-WRAPPED	Victoria Gordon	
NOT SUCH A STRANGER	Liza Hadley	
COLOURS OF LOVE	Rosalie Henaghan	
CHECKMATE	Peggy Nicholson	
TOMORROW'S MAN	Sue Peters	
OF RASCALS AND RAINBOWS	Marcella Thompson	

If you would like to order these books in addition to your regular subscription from Mills & Boon Reader Service please send £1.80 per title to: Mills & Boon Reader Service, Freepost, P.O. Box 236, Croydon, Surrey, CR9 9EL, quote your Subscriber No:................................. (If applicable) and complete the name and address details below. Alternatively, these books are available from many local Newsagents including W.H.Smith, J.Menzies, Martins and other paperback stockists from 5 November 1993.

Name:..

Address:..

....Post Code:.......................

To Retailer: If you would like to stock M&B books please contact your regular book/magazine wholesaler for details.

You may be mailed with offers from other reputable companies as a result of this application. If you would rather not take advantage of these opportunities please tick box ☐